Daughter of Isis

DAUGHTER OF ISIS

A Novel Of The Egyptian Renaissance

Lilian Nirupa

iUniverse, Inc.
New York Lincoln Shanghai

Daughter of Isis

iUniverse books may be ordered through booksellers or by contacting:

iUniverse
2021 Pine Lake Road, Suite 100
Lincoln, NE 68512
www.iuniverse.com
1-800-Authors (1-800-288-4677)

ISBN: 978-0-595-45682-6 (pbk)

ISBN: 978-0-595-69865-3 (cloth)

ISBN: 978-0-595-89984-5 (ebk)

Printed in the United States of America

Preface

The Middle East has witnessed the birth of many civilizations. It has also been the cradle of many clashes of cultures. About 3000 years ago, the Egyptian empire extended from the Sudan to the Mediterranean Sea. For several thousand years this one superpower dominated the whole region. It was the epicenter of culture, military power, stability, refinement, and wealth for the civilized world of the times.

Nothing remains of this magnificent civilization other than its mysterious monuments, profusely illustrated with literature and pictures that reflect every aspect of their rich lives. The most famous and admired are the pyramids of Giza and the Sphinx. They are both symbols of the ancient Egyptians and their successful ecosystem based on geography, religion, tradition, and adherence to the concept of *ma'at*, the Egyptian word for harmony. They also had outstanding knowledge of magic and spiritual understanding, which is still the basis of several modern esoteric traditions.

By the end of the 21st dynasty, this magnificent kingdom was threatened by very disturbing forces from both inside and outside the Kingdom. The Nubians, the Hittites, the Assyrians, and the incipient Greek kingdoms, as well as the "sea peoples" or Mediterranean nomads were jealous of the Empire of the Pharaohs. They conspired with internal rebellious priests trying to undermine the authority of the Pharaoh, the God King who symbolized unity and peace.

Although based in real names, settings and historical circumstances, this is a work of fiction.
Lizla is a brave and beautiful princess whose destiny is to save her beloved country from division and chaos. She is also very psychic, and her spiritual experiences provide guidance, wisdom, and subtle but intense initiation into the ways of love, beauty, spiritual awakening, political power, and friendship.

The times called for much understanding of different traditions, as the beacon of Egyptian wisdom attracted students and teachers, together with spies and traitors, to the increasingly unsettling political scene. The princess learns about diversity and the interaction of body and soul training that inspires her spirituality. The troubling circumstances propel her initiation into romance and intrigue. Her ultimate purpose is given to her by the goddess Isis herself: to discover the ancient mysteries that stood at the root of Egyptian culture and were the basis for their wisdom and knowledge. This book depicts the princess's preparation for this fascinating mission as well as her initiation into the mysteries in her own heart.

Chapter 1

Desert Trials and Rebirth

1,000 BC—Memphis, Lower Egypt.

Lizla opened her eyes and screamed in terror. Complete blackness surrounded her. Had she become blind? Where were the flowers, the lights, the radiant faces she had grown accustomed to holding in almost breathless admiration? Nothing but blackness, thick, like a heavy mourning veil. It even seemed real to the touch. The thought of a mourning veil sent darts of panic up her spine. But wasn't she alive? Wasn't her eager spirit more youthful than ever in her limbs? Her mouth still carried an aftertaste of that exquisite wine that—how did he call himself? Her twin *Ka* (guardian angel)—had given her as a farewell. She tried to remember more, but couldn't. Her memories were being swallowed by anxiety.

She raised her hand and tried to feel the impenetrable surroundings. Beyond the silky robe that covered her body, the air was cool and moist. A penetrating fragrance of myrrh and moss met her approval as her exploring hand reached the clear sensation of—rocks! Yes, it was stone. She searched now, openly with both arms outstretched. In the darkness, she explored as far as she could reach, tracing out a rocky alcove, which surrounded her body about two feet beyond the soft cushion on which she lay. It was rock all the way up to the … She could not touch the zenith of the alcove. Somehow above her, at the distance of her extended arms, there was nothing but the thickness of an implacable darkness.

"It is not a coffin," Lizla thought, trying to keep herself alert and centered. Her own scream had produced a terrifying effect on her nerves. She would not scream again, she warned herself. It was to no avail. Worse than that, there was no echo!

No. She would lie quietly, try to control herself and remember. Perhaps she was dreaming. But no, this was no ordinary circumstance. Nothing in the last two months had been ordinary. Why should it be? Wasn't the full moon of the height of her fourteenth year the appointed time? A time that she and her guides had kept secret from everyone; even from Mother? Why? The question burned again in her mind. Why? She had always confided in Mother. Even in her queenly role, Mother had always found time for Lizla. The late Pharaoh's wife knew the priests had selected her daughter for some special study but the Queen did not interfere. No one interfered with the priests of Amon-Ra. The Pharaoh himself obliged them.

Lizla remembered asking Rat-Ta, her mentor, about the silence regarding her mother. The priest had answered cryptically: "When you awake, the moon shall be no more."

But Lizla's studies had carried her far enough that she could understand "Moon" for "Mother." She remembered asking anxiously: "Will she die?"

The priest had looked at her with compassionate eyes but then answered dryly: "Not in the way you know" and returned to his habitual silence.

She felt calm after a while. She was used to wakeful nights. During the last two months she had spent several vigils on the desert. Ah! But those were different, watching the silver boat of the moon sail among the stars through the pleats of her linen tent …

The coolness of the air and its extreme quietness provided a good cushion for comforting rest. She observed that in musing about the last few weeks of desert training, she had almost forgotten about her strange imprisonment. She realized, rather to her surprise, that her absence of panic was something new. She felt calm, assured—almost content. At that moment she heard steps. No voices. Suddenly the invisible ceiling above her opened into a flash of blue and gold. She recognized the impeccable light of the desert sun on a cloudless sky.

The beloved face of Ra-Ta, her mentor and guide, was illumined with one of his rare smiles. Lizla thought she could read his mind, asking her, "Are you awake?"

He helped her out and invited her to sit on a white silk litter. Two young priestesses of the inner temple carried an almost transparent veil, with which they silently and almost reverently covered Lizla. Through this veil of sky-blue tint, Lizla contemplated the scene as the small caravan departed through the desert noiselessly in a northeasterly direction.

Almost an hour passed. The fiery heat of the desert landscape was soothed away from her eyes by the veil. Ra-Ta had said no word to her. She did not feel like talking either. The familiar landscape took on a dreamy aspect which combined with her newly discovered calmness. Lizla reflected on this and was puzzled again. Scarcely three months ago she was running around with her cousins, Allen and Ten-pa, and the strange blue-eyed Mikos. Then Mikos had disappeared and Mizzia had come. Mother approved of Mizzia, the dark-eyed, witty Babylonian girl who served in Aunt Lillie's nursery. Together, Lizla and Mizzia had spent many hours roaming around Aunt Lillie's magnificent apartments and trying her perfumes, veils, oils and gowns. Princess Lillie was a widow, but young and beautiful. Many young pretenders were trying to win her attention. A year after her husband's death, her life was a succession of parties and ceremonies, which Lillie attended arrayed in splendid clothes and elaborate coiffures.

All of that was in the past, though—childish things from a childish past, Lizla reflected rather gravely. Mother had suggested something about her impending womanhood and the changes it would bring.

But when Lizla had commented on this subject to Ra-Ta, he had turned serious and had parted abruptly. That very night she had been informed that her desert trials were to be initiated.

But now, she remembered, Mizzia had also said something about womanly changes when they had confided in each other that full-moon night of the Springtime Festival.

Lizla remembered Mizzia's figure, tall and slender, moving so gracefully under the olive branches of Princess Lillie's garden. That beautiful night! It was unusually hot, and the sweet music of harps and lutes and the rustle of the papyri vines added to the enchanting flavor of the wine and honey, the smell of which mingled with the lotus flower oil that ran through her hair. Lizla had always loved lotus perfume. That evening, the small perfume cone, made of the purest wax, imbued with lotus perfume oil, had almost saturated her hair and gown as the two girls danced gaily through the garden. Then they had rested, sitting by the rectangular pool, and they talked and drank more wine and ate figs and honey cakes. They had seen Princess Lillie disappear behind a vine-covered gazebo, accompanied by Mikos's older brother Lizla had wanted to run after them and ask the tall, handsome Greek about his younger brother, but Mizzia had stopped her. It was then that Mizzia had confided her strange story. Her eyes were bright with wine and mirth and a newfound mischievous glint, which Mizzia had tried to disguise from her wide-eyed younger friend. Lizla could sense Mizzia's blushing under the bright moonlight as she told her about her past.

"It was another full moon, like this," she had begun. She told of a strong, tall, dark Assyrian man who had taken her by the river after a night of wine and merriment at the Harvest Feast. His hands, burning with passion, had held her trembling hands and his full lips tasted of wine and honey as they met hers. In the moonlight his eyes had shone like fiery coals. His eyes and hers closed under the magic pressure of passion and, Mizzia concluded, "He took me into the darkness." She had stopped talking then, her eyes, her whole frame vacant, as if her soul were lost in her memories.

Lizla watched, puzzled, holding her breath. When Mizzia came back to the present, she added melancholically, "I never saw him again. He went with a caravan to Egypt. Five moons later, I knew I was with child. My old aunt helped me out. Her oldest son was going to Egypt and took me as a slave, so he said. My father was away and my stepmother was glad to be rid of the problem. My child was born on the way and died. We were attacked by nomads."

Mizzia ended her story, saying that she was sold to the Vizier. His son took a liking to her, but the Vizier was wise; he gave her as a gift to Princess Lillie. Mizzia was happy there. She loved the children and praised her gods for being placed in the palace.

Lizla's memories were the only things stirring on this quiet trip across the desert. But she wouldn't talk. She knew that aspect of her training was very important. Silence, inner and outer silence, her mentor had imposed. Besides her calmness, another factor began crystallizing in her mind as a new realization. She could almost guess what Ra-Ta was thinking—when he was thinking about her. It had proved true over and over again, these past two months. It was something she used to dream about often, when she was a child. She used to dream that she was in one of those large boats going through the Nile on a hunting trip and everybody would talk, sometimes not saying the truth, but she could "see" their hearts and what they really meant, and it was no disturbance to her. Later on, when not dreaming, if she happened to guess what people thought or foresaw their intentions, she felt quite startled about it, as if something was not right with her.

It was different now. She knew almost instinctively what Ra-Ta was thinking by his eyes and his movements. She felt she could almost read his body and see his thoughts, but even that realization didn't surprise her or alarm her anymore.

Her thoughts turned to Mikos, the blue-eyed Greek boy who had disappeared three months ago. Lizla and Mikos had become good friends in spite of his shyness. Lizla loved to tease him on that account. Once Mikos had found a snakeskin and told her a strange story about snakes changing skins and leaving their old ones behind.

Perhaps that was what had happened to her. She wondered where her old skin was. Maybe she had left it in the dark. Maybe … The dark! Mizzia had gone into the dark too. Would she, Lizla, have a baby too? Was that the way serpents are born? Or humans?

Lizla felt confused by the strange experience of calmness in her heart while her mind was whirling with random memories. She suddenly felt so ignorant. It was most unusual for an Egyptian girl to go to school—almost impossible, unless she was a princess like Lizla herself—a heir to the throne—or if the stars indicated something special about her destiny. Ra-Ta had said something about it. The peasants did not study, for, as he would say, the spirits took care of the ordinary people's known and their unknowns, while whatever they personally could control was ruled by law and tradition. But people in government were different. The gods left more options open to them, but in spite of their privileged birth, many nobles and princes did not "wake up" for they forgot their higher destiny. Ra-Ta did not say more, but Lizla knew what he was thinking. As far as he was concerned, these ignorant aristocrats were more brutes than the peasants. They did nothing but party and change wives, hunt and drink. Any scribe copying the taxes inventory for the Pharaoh or the Temple was more worthy than they were.

He had said, however, that sometimes the peasant girls could "wake up", but Lizla should keep away from them since they were witches. Eventually these peasant girls' overheated vision would drive them along by the mortuary homes where the evil spirits would possess them and loose them in the desert to dry their blood in the sun—-for that's what happens to the blood when it catches fire through untrained awakening. For the first time this morning Lizla remembered that with uneasiness. Somehow it did not ring true; she wondered if maybe he told her that to protect her somehow … She wondered why; she had never doubted her teacher's words before. What had happened to her under the sand?

Lizla was not sure which destiny the stars had marked for her. All she knew was that she had been chosen, and that training was very important. It could mean the difference between life and death or even worse, madness, which drives one's "*Ka*" or individual soul wild until it gets lost into the heavy worlds of the lower spirits.

The caravan approached the sunset as it ended. The glories of the desert made its best display when the rich, foamy clouds arrayed themselves in gold and pink to salute the Sun god Ra's departure beneath the horizon. But that was at their back. At the east, against a deep blue-indigo sky, the immaculate whiteness of the Isis temple emerged in the midst of a heavenly garden of date palms and flowing fountains.

An array of maidens dressed in white linen—whose black shoulder-length hair contrasted vividly with the bronze of their skins and the gold of their bracelets and waistbands—saluted the exit of Ra with a soft lullaby of papyrus vines and melancholy lutes. They smiled dreamily to the small group as it made the entrance into the back portal of the Temple of Isis.

Ra-Ta gently took her hand and helped her out of the litter. They entered noiselessly through the Western portal, into a painted corridor where a series of doors indicated the presence of more rooms, the incensed perfumed apartments of the Isis priestesses.

Ra-Ta gently took the veil away from Lizla and looked once again at her loveliness. Dark-dreamy eyes, large and lustrous, adorned her round clear face, soft like the full moon. Her black hair contrasted with the pale tint of her complexion, and shadows under her eyes also reminded him of the severe training of fasting and vigils she had taken on so valiantly. She had lost some weight, too, and her tall slender figure reminded him of a papyrus vine, rendered graceful and agile by the daily exercise of the sacred dances. He thought about her chart. Yes, she had been born by the end of the winter. A Pisces sun heralded her prophetic destiny. Capricorn rising, her queenly future and the enigmatic moon in Aquarius, sign of the dreamers, opposed her proud Leo Venus. The dart in the heart of the mystics! Ah, but a fiery Venus could "wake up" early in the sense of the flesh. That's why he had precipitated her training into the mysteries when he heard the

Queen's intention of giving her to the influence of her Babylonian young friend's worldly knowledge. She would have time for that.

Isis should be her mother. She would train her in the mysteries of the soul and womanhood at the same time, like a real Queen—like the Priestess she was born to be. Yes, he had acted on time! And it was working, he could tell! The two young priestesses took Lizla by the hand and led her to a small chamber. Its intimate beauty touched Lizla. The white walls were covered partially with a large fresco of Isis, rescuing Osiris from the Nile. A light blue curtain that was drawn open to show the picture covering the rest of the walls. Lizla wondered if they had left it open only for her. Soon she was left alone.

A small table with refreshments of figs, dates, and honey cakes was there and an alabaster jug with pink wine was on the table. Lizla took a small silver cup and filled it with pink wine. The taste startled her. Its sweetness reminded her of something … She took a date and chewed it. The sweetness intensified. Reclining on the silky cushioned chair, she closed her eyes. The scent of jasmine in two tall vases by the sides of a picture filled the room with an almost mystical atmosphere. As she put the silver cup back on the table, she noticed a small inscription embossed in hieroglyphics: "To the sweetness of Love."

"What an appropriate toast," she thought. She closed her eyes again and rose into Meditation. Soon she was deep in trance. As the soft breeze on her forehead intensified, Lizla awoke. She was surprised to find herself alone. No windows or slaves were there to move a fan. She felt good, although a little cold. At that moment Ra-Ta, accompanied by the two young priestesses, came for her. She was led through long corridors magnificently painted with murals of the life of Isis, Osiris, and Horus. At the end of the corridor, they stood at a door that was exceedingly small in comparison with the rest of the building, where the ceiling of the corridor was the height of ten men. The white door had no other ornament but a cross of life in relief above which—also in white relief—the letters were inscribed in the priestly language of hieroglyphics: REBIRTH CHAMBER.

The young priestess at Ra-Ta's right presented him with a small box of deep blue silk. Ra-Ta opened it and extracted a golden key. Lizla felt a chill run up her spine. Was she going to have a baby?

The door opened and the young priestesses quietly but diligently turned on a huge golden lamp in the shape of an alabaster angel. The hands of this ten-foot-tall figure were held together at chest level as if making an offering. The angel carried a plate of alabaster fruits. Figs, grapes, and pomegranates were so finely shaped that when the oil in its highest center was lit; its light produced an amber glow that seemed to emanate from the angel's heart.

The rest of the angel's shape, except the wings and hair that were of fine gold, was of the same amber-colored alabaster, so when a second lamp was lit on a crown above his head, the light flowed down the pleats of his ankle-long tunic, as if the finger of a god had showered heavenly light upon it. Opposite the angel was a throne, a large and imposing chair, whose back formed the golden statue of Horus, its hawk head rising above the height of a sitting person's head. The young priestesses helped Lizla sit down on the throne and then, with the same graceful speed at which they had been moving since entering the chamber, they left.

Ra-Ta spoke for the first time since Lizla could remember after he had led her out of her strange entombment in the desert. "Lie down, please," he said softly, pointing to a golden button at Lizla's right. She pressed the button on the arm of the throne and the chair opened up into a couch of soft blue linen. The movement had been so gentle, Lizla wasn't even startled. For all she knew it could have been Ra-Ta's magic. But she had seen recliners before, although more rustic both in shape and movement.

"I want you to close your eyes and do exactly as I tell you."

The unnecessary recommendation put Lizla on the alert. He knew of her ability and obedience.

"There is nothing to fear," Ra-Ta had read her thoughts. "What you will experience will hopefully awaken you. I believe you are prepared, but only Isis knows her daughters."

Despite the solemnity of the occasion, Lizla couldn't avoid a faint smile. It was the first time Ra-Ta had mentioned anything about his apprehensions of training a woman.

As Ra-Ta initiated the Isis invocation, Lizla felt a sweet stream of peace flowing up her body. Her eyelids closed, erasing the image of the angel's eyes, where the light on the mind and the heart seemed to converge into mysterious tenderness.

The priest guided Lizla through the rhythmic breathing exercises that constituted the driving force of the Egyptian rebirth procedure. A pressure in her heart made Lizla pause to rest.

The voice of Ra-Ta was soft but firm: "Keep on breathing."

Then there was a sharp pain beneath her ribs with a suffocating feeling. Another pause followed. His voice stern but reassuring, Ra-Ta held her arm, applying pressure at some specific points to control anxiety. An hour passed. Lizla felt the life of her nerves reverberate with vitality, as one by one her power blockages were released. Lizla's breathing accelerated, and her whole frame vibrated with energy. She saw waves of golden lights running like fire up and down her limbs, and her spine seemed to stretch out into a bright white-bluish light that cascaded into her head. A feeling of sheer delight accompanied that climax and as she relaxed (she was allowed to do so—no more orders for breathing) the golden light started rippling off and out, inundating her consciousness of the room, the temple, and the world. Waves and waves of golden light kept spreading out and away, while again she felt the taste of an exquisite wine on the tip of her tongue. She remembered her twin-*Ka* and oh! The dream! Yes, it was a dream she had experienced while she was underground. She remembered now. She had been given a strong herb tea prepared by one of the young priestesses, and she had fallen asleep in the sun. How had she wakened in the darkness like that? Somehow it did not matter now. Her feeling of ecstasy was complete. The eyes of her twin-*Ka* seemed to flood her consciousness with the honey-wine taste. The vision smiled and said: "Watch your teacher's movements."

Lizla had almost forgotten about Ra-Ta. Ra-Ta was smiling, a knowing smile, the experiment was proving to be excellent. Lizla's aura had the most brilliant colors, like the rainbow but infinitely more brilliant. And a halo of white light hovered above her head. The white light! Ah! For how long it would still hover above the head of the elected. What had the prophecy said? One thousand times more should the earth go through the twelve constellations! One thousand years more before the Prince of Peace would come and bring down the gift of the white light into the hearts of the faithful.

Ra-Ta was interrupted in his musings by a sigh from his beloved disciple.

He replied, "Watch my hands now—no! Don't open your eyes. Just feel them." He placed his right hand about two inches above her forehead. "Can you feel it?"

"Yes," answered Lizla very quietly. Without touching her, Ra-Ta ran his left hand up and down above Lizla's aura, again at a distance of about two inches. In the area between her waist and her legs he felt a "hole" of energy, a cool spot. He could feel himself re-energized by the incredible powerful vibrations Lizla was emanating. He stopped his hand at that spot.

"Daughter of the Light, can you answer?"

She was still floating in the golden light, but in her inner vision, she saw clouds of dust and among them a chariot pulled by two bright white horses. A young man was in the chariot. She could not see his face. She strove to see through the dust clouds …

Ra-Ta repeated the question; "Daughter of the Light, can you hear me? What do you see?"

Lizla answered, "I see a man in a chariot." Ra-Ta raised his brows almost against his will. He had suspected that. The spot that had been cool, just above her womb, started to feel like whirlpools of cold and hot air currents.

"What does he look like, can you see his face?"

"He's wrapped in clouds of dust," Lizla replied. Ra-Ta smiled approvingly. "He looks like, he is—oh, yes—it's Mikos. In a chariot! He had disappeared, didn't you know? Did he go to war?" Lizla's voice kept on coming different levels of speed, out of her trance vision.

Ra-Ta answered softly, "To war? No! What colors are his horses?"

"White, brilliant white; he also has a white light hovering above his head. Oh! Is he dead?" The whirlpools above her womb accelerated intensely.

"No," said the teacher. "Don't worry, he is fine. Did he look at you?"

Lizla's lips tried to mumble and answer, but did not part. Ra-Ta sighed to himself in resignation. He moved his hand to her waist level. He realized there the current in her aura was firm and strong; he could even feel the golden color.

"Daughter of the Light, what do you see?"

Lizla took a deep breath, filling her whole body with light and power. "I see a queen on a throne."

"Do you see her face?" Ra-Ta asked.

"No, I cannot, she is veiled. But I can tell she is powerful, and beautiful, and she has tears in her eyes. She has a weight on her heart. It's her people, there is hunger and war—yes," Lizla's voice kept coming, hesitatingly. "There is war and her children are fighting … But she is strong and brave …"

Ra-Ta nodded approvingly. He was aware of that. Ra-Ta tried a last experiment. Moving his hand directly above her heart, he asked again, "Daughter of the Light, what can you see?

"A chain, a chain of gold and roses. And a finger—it's working on the chain."

"Can you see the finger's owner?" Ra-Ta asked tremulously.

"Yes, it is Horus. It's unlocking the chain."

Ra-Ta felt a lump in his throat. What a blessing from the god of wisdom! And to a woman! It was enough. The girl should rest now. Her trials were over for the present.

Quietly, he instructed his disciple to return to the physical world through gentle but grounding breathing exercises. Lizla finally took a deep breath with a deep sigh and then opened her eyes. They shone like two jewels.

CHAPTER 2

ISIS MEETS HER DAUGHTER

The morning came through the palm trees of the eastern dunes. It smelled of sand, dates, and summertime, Lizla thought as she wet her hand in the large swimming pool by the temple. She had enjoyed a deep night's sleep, with no dreams, and her body felt so full of energy!

Ra-Ta had not seen her yet. Again, last night he had recommended silence, although she was ordered to remember her vision before trying to fall asleep and to offer those memories to Isis. She had slept in the same room where the beautiful picture of Isis and Osiris was. As she closed her eyes for the evening meditation, the images of the three visions had come to her mind. She knew what they meant. Some parts of her body, like any human body, contained centers of power. There were seven of them in the physical and nine in the *Ka*. She had visions on the second, third, and fourth center. They meant creativity/children, personal power or government, and human love/emotion. So she had learned; so it had to be. She had felt and seen those centers before, like burning wheels, in her desert meditations.

But then she remembered how last night, in her quiet bedroom as she offered her images to Isis, the Goddess had answered her. She had felt a very distinct presence, like a globe of pale rose, very powerful and vibrant, arise upon her heart.

The sweet face of Isis had said with musical accents, "I accept you as my child. After your morning bath, come to me for instructions."

Then Lizla had fallen asleep, quiet, fulfilled, and contented for the first time since her departure from the palace. Strange as her destiny might be, it was a sure path. It made sense. Unconsciously, she drew the quiet confidence that custom and tradition provide, no matter how strange the grounds. Her unusual experiences still had a deep, serene, loving, and life-giving Egyptian background. Like the rich gold setting of a precious stone, mystic traditions provide some cushion of comfort, a refuge from the formidable winds that the awakening of souls requires.

Taking her left sandal off, she dipped her gracefully shaped foot into the water. It was cool, but gentle. She was used to the bitter cold of the desert nights. With a brisk movement, she let her shoulder pins loose, and her gown fell to the floor. She thought she was alone, but behind the olive trees that protected the pool from the desert sands, a silent presence was watching very intently the supple movements of her slender nude body slipping into the water. It was Psusennes, the lion hunter. A cousin of Lizla, this sports-loving prince had his own palace by the Nile, about one hundred miles down the river. He smiled approvingly at the gentleness of her movements and the delicate features of her face. But the body was still slim and childish; the well-shaped breasts were not full enough to meet Egyptian standards of womanly beauty. But she was shaping into a woman, he thought, and the proud movements of her head and hands in swimming, and the impeccable harmony of her wholesome body frame, still caught his attention. It would be interesting to see how she developed; he caught himself thinking rather irreverently, as he remembered they were on holy grounds.

He had come here on pilgrimage. His devotion to Isis, the perfect woman—Queen, lover, healer, and mother—was his spiritual image of perfection. Not that he disdained the more imperfect forms of womanhood, as he found them most delightful. His fame as a lover was considerable, but the gentleness of his well-developed masculinity had created some form of a legend for him. In and out of most Egyptian palaces, he was cherished by women and somehow envied by men, but it had never been said that he harmed anyone. Instead, many a wayward princess who went to see his famous zoological garden down the river and stayed in his purple palace had returned with a kinder heart in which to cherish the passionate memories of her romantic adventures with him.

Lizla emerged from the pool out onto the sandy deck, her body still vibrant with the energies of the rebirth experience. She stood arms up, above her head, stretching in the sun, totally unaware of being observed. Psusennes mentally thanked the Goddess for this opportunity to "meet" his cousin. He was almost unconsciously getting a picture of how she would be sculpted into the perfect form of woman. She had all the potential for it. He felt his hands moving accordingly. He stopped himself with a smile. How soon had his youthful cousin taken him!

Lizla put on her gown and sandals and went back to her chamber. The Goddess had said to come in for instructions.

As she entered the room, the jasmine fragrance proved soothing to her spirit. There was something definitely delicate and somehow insinuating of the promise of adventure in the perfume of the jasmine, just like Isis herself.

Lizla bowed before the picture and sat in her chair for meditation. The tall figure of Isis, crowned with the double kingdom crown, was the focus of her attention. As she reverently closed her eyes, Lizla started repeating the Isis invocation.

A pearly cloud of white and pink light overcame her consciousness. In its center, tall, queenly, with a radiant face and an even more luminous smile, the Goddess met her disciple.

"I am Isis. As it was written, you have awakened in my temple, where I led you. You have passed your tests and have become my daughter. From now on you will not call anyone Mother except me."

A radiant aura of perfected womanhood emanated from her. Lotus flowers were on her waist, symbol of spiritual serenity and the deep peace that could only come from the Mother of Horus, the God of Wisdom. Her gown was white with a golden waistband. Her breasts were full and firm, irradiating a life-giving presence. The finest of Egyptian linens were almost translucent as the vision appeared, insinuating a fully developed female form, while making it more apparent than obvious. Her lips, full but delicate, wore a golden copper color which contrasted with the golden tan of her exquisite skin. Her movements were regal, and her voice was imperious and tender all at once.

"Daughter of the Light, you were contemplating my picture. What did you notice most?" Her voice filled the room with music-ripples, vibrations of a joyful peace.

"I saw that you were wearing the crown of the two kingdoms." Lizla answered tremulously.

"You are very perceptive, humble, and obedient for your princely birth. I am pleased with you.

But let me tell you about myself," Isis answered and continued: "Yes, the message of the two crowns was for you to see. As you reflected yesterday, the picture was left intentionally for your meditation and enlightenment. I came to Earth many thousands of years ago, to teach all men and especially women, of the real law—the Law of ONE. ONE is my crown, as one is the greatness of Egypt; ONE is the miraculous fertility of this desert land, united by the One River. The Nile, whose waters have been used, and will be used, for many more thousands of years, will never harm anyone. This life blood of the Egyptian soil has healing qualities, and it unites all men in its fecundate task. ONE is the eternal spirit that rules the three worlds, the One whom all wise men call God. It was to show the magnitude of this one Power that when the forces of the darkness killed and dismembered my husband Osiris, throwing him to the Nile, the strength of my love and our union made Osiris One again. Do you understand all this?"

Lizla nodded reverently. How magnificent Isis looked, and how powerful her words that seemed to expand into Lizla's heart until it felt it would explode out of her chest!

The Goddess continued, "Well, now and in the near future, the oneness of Egypt is once again threatened. The stars mark difficult times for our beloved land. The illusions of selfish ambition and separation will bring pain and drought, war and famine to our country. And you will have a healing part in it—with my aid, of course."

"Me?" Lizla's heart started pounding heavily.

"Yes. It will be most important for many of our people and eventually the people of other lands and even other times. Egypt must be one. The time will come, one thousand years from now, that the Prince of Peace will come to Earth. He will find refuge in our peace during his childhood and later being initiated into the Law of One that you will re-discover.

Division has brought destruction in the past. That past contained many, now lost, sacred secrets of the wisdom of the ancient sages from whom our civilization evolved. Those treasured sacred texts must be recovered. They were saved for crisis times, like the one coming. Your gifts and your crown—yes, you will reign someday—can help immeasurably. But it will mean pain for you and struggle, sometimes bitter and cruel struggle. You do not *have* to do this. With your gifts and your nature, you can stay in the temple and remain isolated from the events to come. No, don't answer me now. Tomorrow you will have a day alone by the Nile. Do not talk to anyone. Let the Nile and your heart talk to each other. Then you will come back to me and give me your answer. In the meantime, you have my blessings."

With that, the Goddess disappeared, leaving Lizla alone with her puzzled thoughts.

Lizla spent the rest of the day accompanied by Iris and Ila-Re, the two young priestesses that had been with her during the rebirthing preparation. Together they explored the different facilities of the

Temple of Isis. It was located southwest of the capital city of the province, at a distance of about eighty miles. The grounds were large, several hundred acres, and it combined the different aspects of the Isis Mysteries. A healing center was dedicated to women, where childbirth preparation and delivery were conducted for the priestly families and the noble classes, although, on occasion, ordinary citizens were received when a doctor interceded for a patient. The religious study center and the Mysteries were closed to the public as well as the Inner Temple, which only the Elected could enter. The Temple Beautiful and the Temple of Love were dedicated to the development and refinement of the different arts of femininity, which the Egyptians had developed extensively. Classes in art, incense preparation, dance-exercises, the making of candles, incense, perfumes, cosmetics, body reconstructing, and swimming were conducted by special priestesses, who had dedicated their lives to the development of excellence in womanhood and to sacrifice to Isis.

Trying to keep her thoughts away from the morning experience, Lizla found the grounds fascinating. The food was excellent, well balanced by the famous beauticians who made the princesses of Egypt famous worldwide.

By the evening, she saw Ra-Ta again, and to him she confided her strange experience. He listened to her and was deeply moved. So the Goddess had special plans for his disciple! He was honored to be an instrument of it. He also felt fascinated by the prospect of discovering the writings of the Ancients. He had heard a lot about them. Regarding the political problems, he frowned and thought to himself: that was the way of the world. That was one of the blessings of belonging to the priesthood. In spite of the strong political influence they had on the Pharaoh and the court, they were spared direct involvement with worldly affairs … They acted as counselors and then could retire. Personally, he preferred it that way.

But he would never try to influence Lizla in her choice. The Goddess was right. How had she said it? "It would be between the Nile and her heart." Strange were the ways of women, even the heavenly ones. He sighed and rose to open the door, as he heard knocking. He was pleasantly surprised to see the athletic figure of Psusennes. He was one of the largest donors to the temple. Many beautiful things had been done through his support.

The prince entered and bowed to the Priest, requesting his blessings. Then he simulated surprise to see his cousin Lizla. She had not seen him for a long time, although she had heard stories of his magnificent palace. With her own father she had visited his famous zoological garden when she was a child. Lizla felt his eyes scrutinizing her figure and her face a little too daringly.

Answering his salute with a proud good night and bowing to her master, she departed.

Ah, Ra-Ta!" Psusennes started after she left. "When did you cultivate that beautiful flower?"

Ra-Ta looked at him with an all-knowing look. "Leave her alone, my prince, she is just a child."

"Not for long, my reverend priest, not for long. Is she destined for the priesthood?" he asked incredulously.

"We do not know yet. She went through her rebirthing yesterday," Ra-Ta answered.

"Rebirthing a woman so young? Who is she?" Psusennes was now quite puzzled.

"Ah, my prince, there are some things I cannot tell even you, not for now, anyhow. By the way, what brings you here at this time? It is lion hunting season."

"False alarm, my dear Priest, false alarm. I've got the wrong news. Altamira," he smiled.

The priest nodded. Altamira and Psusennes were the latest story running through most palatial corridors lately.

Psusennes continued, "Well, I've heard she was with child and looking ill, but it was a false alarm. She is with child, all right, but she still looks adorable. I can't wait to see her again, free and joyful, in her childlike playful dancing." He restrained himself from speaking further. Ra-Ta was one of the highest priests; one of the ten who held the

Key to the Mysteries. Even a privileged prince like Psusennes had to revere his holiness.

Ra-Ta had other thoughts too. He did not believe in coincidences. The Goddess had brought Lizla and Psusennes together at this time. Ra-Ta wondered why … In any case, Ra-Ta felt he did not have to wait for the morning to know Lizla's decision about accepting her destiny in her nation's future. He had lived long enough to see the finger of fate pointing in the right direction.

Chapter 3

The Vision of the Nile

The morning had arrived in splendid clear skies. Lizla took a deep breath in and mentally murmured the celebrated Ra invocation to the rising sun. Religion had never been a mere duty to her. The life of the soul was very present in her consciousness, partly because of her psychic nature. Religion was deeply ingrained in the daily life of Egyptians in general, since they were quite aware of the underlying patterns of energy that move and protect all things. They called them spirits. They were the spirits of the planets, of the plants, of the rocks, of the Nile, of the animals—and of course, each human being had his or her *Ka*, a psychic double and soul.

Life was compounded of visible and invisible realities which interacted in a rhythmic dance, like the waters of the Nile refreshed the desert, and the heat of the sun evaporated the waters, yielding three harvests of wheat a year. Life was sacred, and death was another form of life whose entrance was celebrated like a trip into another world. Provisions, furniture, and companionship were planned and arranged for the trip into the next world through elaborate ceremonies. The rich and powerful invested heavily in mortuary preparations during their lifetimes, and no victory or accomplishment was considered complete if its history was not recorded in the tomb of its author. This thirst for immortality made the presence of the gods very real for the average Egyptian, man or woman. They loved life, family, and the fatherland passionately. Even among the powerful, travel abroad was considered a burden, and existence in another country the most disgraceful thing that could happen to one: Exhile!

The natural rhythm of heaven and earth, river and land, gods and people, rich and poor, intermingled like the four seasons. This contributed to a rich and harmonious environment wherein life was to be cherished and its secrets to be unfolded as in few civilizations before, or even after them. The wisdom of Egypt held universal fame, and many learned men from other cultures and even other ages would draw from them the basis for their mysteries and occult knowledge.

After a brief and silent breakfast, Lizla took a small bowl with some fruits and flowers for the noon offering. Then, accompanied by two slaves who carried her in a litter, she departed for the Nile.

She arrived there in about an hour. After giving orders to them to pick her up at sunset, she decided to walk about the river's bank. She walked along the river until she saw a small caravan that had stopped to refresh.

A little girl of about four years old was standing in the water, and her eyes seemed lost in thought as her father intoned the grateful invocation to the Nile god. Lizla had a flashback to early childhood, when her own father had stood by the Nile, invoking the all-beneficent god. She had seen the Nile's god in her mind's eye, just like her grandmother described him. It had been a glorious ceremony, as her father was the last Pharaoh, who later died valiantly in the victorious war against the oppressive Assyrians. Her uncle reigned now, but her family still held a royal position in the palace. That grayish morning by the riverbank, she had beheld the image of the god. He had no face of stone. His sculpture was forbidden, but it was believed he possessed a man's body with female breasts, symbolizing the fertility he provided to the land. Her grandmother had described him as the blood of the earth, and his mother-father figure had impressed strongly upon Lizla's imagination. Then she had stood by the river, watching her small feet turning pale under the water, and as the ripples came and went, her own feet seemed to lose consistency and reality, like the invisible god of the father-mother river. She felt one with the river, one with the blood of the land. She felt a child of the river, sharing his/her life. She felt flowing through her own blood the river with his/her enormous power to give, to create, and to destroy.

Watching that little girl standing by the river opened another insight in Lizla's learning adventure. How much her knowledge had expanded in the last few weeks! That was what the Goddess had said. Let the river talk to her heart. But she was a little girl no longer.

At that moment, a cry of terror burst like an icy dagger into her consciousness. A small child, playing with ripples, had gone too far, and a crocodile had caught her tiny arm. The mother cried loudly. Father and mother, forgetting the danger, threw themselves into the river, ignoring the group of crocodiles that had gathered to the smell of blood. Armed with rustic farm tools, they fought desperately against the six or seven beasts in a bloody battle. Lizla felt frozen on the spot momentarily. The mother managed to rescue the little one, while a group of fishermen armed with stones fought bravely, taking the wounded man to the shore and succeeding in sending the rest of the beasts away.

Lizla forgot about her former musings. Jumping to help, she found the man badly wounded on both arms. There was too much heart among the Egyptians to allow differences of classes to dismiss the suffering of the poor. She had seen Pharaoh go out of his way many times to provide for a faithful servant. (She had also seen him kill mercilessly a traitor or thief, and his whole family murdered and dismembered when they incurred his wrath.)

Today this fisherman's valiant act moved Lizla to act quickly. She took off the veil of linen cloth she wore to cover her hair from the morning mist and tore it into small strips to use as bandages. Then she emptied her fruit box, putting the contents on a small pile of sand. She approached the small group that surrounded the wounded man, who was lying on the beach. Her royal bearing and the clarity of her skin announced her as a noble. They let her through. She had learned the rudiments of healing in her early training. She also remembered the Goddess talking about the healing properties of the Nile waters. Lizla herself, having divine Pharaoh's blood, was considered part of the family of the gods. So, armed with faith and compassion, she approached the valiant man. He could hardly breathe with pain, but he pointed first to the child. Lizla took a look at both. The child had been lucky. His small arms, well-oiled by a dutiful mother, as was the custom, had been barely bruised and only scraped by the crocodile's paw. He was an excellent swimmer and had given the beast a good hard time in trying to seize him again. The man was different: his right arm and left leg had fallen prey to the crocodile's teeth. As for his left leg, Lizla did not say, but she feared amputation would be required. She cleaned and washed the wounds of both the child and father, and gave them some grapes and figs. Then, ordering the rest of the caravan to proceed with their normal routine, she stood by the ailing man, promising to take him to the Temple's hospital as soon as he had rested some. Kneeling by the side of the man, she closed his grateful eyes and ordered him to rest, putting an end to his litany of blessings and praises to the gods for saving his family.

She laid her hand on the man's forehead, underneath which, Ra-Ta had taught her, was man's inner vision center. Then she put another hand on his chest to calm his nerves. As she closed her eyes, she repeated the Invocation to Isis, mother-healer. A warm, pink glow covered them both. In a few minutes, the man was sleeping. She bandaged the wounds as well as she could.

Lizla went to the river to wash her hands and came back to the man's side. There she sat on the brownish sand to ponder and rest.

She had come to find an answer to the Goddess, and what had she found? A deep, serene glow of contentment, partly from the glory of

Isis's presence and the gentle fire of healing love that her hands still felt. The river had given her a new lesson, just as when she was a child. A family forgetting their personal safety, just thinking of one another, the healing of the river, the Goddess's love and wisdom, and the deep contentment of her heart told her what to do. If the stars gave her an opportunity to be a healer to her country, that was what her heart desired. She would tell the Goddess, "Yes!"

She finally felt hungry. She stretched out in the sand and reached for the rest of her fruit. Contemplating the soft ripples of the Nile coming on the shore, she finished her lunch quietly, thanking her *Ka* both for her meal and for the wise solution to her problem. Taking a small bookcase from her box, she wrote a few lines. Then she rose to her feet and called two young boys who were playing on the beach.

"Do you want to earn a silver coin?" Lizla asked.

"Really?" Their eyes shone incredulously.

"Do you know where the temple of Isis, is?"

"Yes, we do, princess." They both bowed as they answered reverently. That was well-known as privileged ground.

"All right, take this message and give it to the guard at the door, and I will give you the coin."

The boys departed with exhilaration.

Half an hour later, two slaves carrying a palanquin and accompanied by Ra-Ta arrived with two litters. They accommodated the sleeping man on one and the mother and children in the other, as the boy was wounded and the mother was with child.

Before Ra-Ta could ask her any questions, Lizla, without any formalities, communicated to him both the events of the day and her decision to accept the Goddess's plea. It was considered impolite to talk to the teacher without being addressed, but Ra-Ta listened calmly as usual, noting with satisfaction her unusual excitement.

Ra-Ta was a gifted and experienced astrologer as well as a renowned teacher. He knew enough about Lizla to understand her feelings, but he still was amazed at the extent of her gifts.

"How did you put him to sleep? Did you have a sedative?" He asked her.

She answer plainly, "No, I just laid my hand on his head for vision and my other hand on his heart for calmness and invoked the name of Isis. It didn't occur to me about a sedative. I was just listening to my *Ka*."

Listening to one's *Ka*, or psychic double, was a way of inner atonement that was widespread in Egypt. The word "la" could refer to a "soul, "spirit, "effective personality," and "effectiveness, glory, and success".

Ra-Ta nodded approvingly. Yes, she had done an excellent job. The Temple had a sizable hospital, as Isis was the magician and healer "par excellence" worldwide; her cults attracted the medicine man in almost all his healing invocations. Under the royal healing auspices, the humble family would find refuge until the man was healed and the woman had delivered her baby.

Lizla took delight in picking up and caressing the little girl, Amura-bel, whom she had found meditating so seriously in the water. On impulse, she asked the mother for her birth date. She would use her case in her astrology classes. Who knows? Sometimes even the peasants could have strange destinies. Ra-Ta frowned, but accepted it. He was still puzzled by the healing powers of his disciple.

Ra-Ta realized that the wounded man's left leg was very bad. It might even have to be amputated. That would be no problem in the Temple. It held the most competent surgeons of the world known at that time. But perhaps it could be saved. His other wounds looked clean, and some restoring could be seen already in the torn tissues. Amazing!

Ra-Ta and Lizla fell into silence as they walked side by side next to the palanquins on their way back to the Temple. They arrived by mid-afternoon and went directly to the hospital. Without delay, three priestesses took care of the wounded man, and a doctor was called in. The woman and children were taken to the guestrooms, which they entered rather timidly as they were not used to so much luxury.

Lizla went to her room with her teacher's blessings. There, before her beloved picture, she sat in meditation. Half an hour passed before her excitement was subdued enough for her to tune in to the higher levels.

There she found her graceful Mother Isis, waiting for her answer.

"Mother, I've decided to follow the destiny the stars have marked for me," Lizla said, her heart glowing with gratitude as she saw the Goddess smiling.

"Very well, then. I think you have made the right decision. But because of it, your training must continue. So much you will accomplish, so much you must learn."

"I would be grateful for that too, Mother. I've noticed that learning has made my life richer in just a few weeks, and I would love to continue. Mother," Lizla's *Ka* was prompting her to seek more. "There is something I saw today, when I helped this man. Do you expect me to heal people?"

"Yes, I noticed with pleasure your delight in that too. A child of mine in my Temple should follow my path, healing and magic. But you will follow my path all the way. You will be a queen; you will help heal your country. And an Egyptian queen must be a WOMAN." The letters seemed to impregnate Lizla's mind like fire. "The queen is a woman equal in power to the Pharaoh, yet she is a woman and favorite in the midst of a harem of the most beautiful women in the world today. Do you see what I mean?" Isis's eyes were compassionate and almost merry. Lizla nodded respectfully but felt a pang of uneasiness creeping into her heart.

"You have no need to worry. Don't forget, it is your destiny. You want succeed, don't you?"

Lizla felt her proud Leo Venus rising to the occasion. "Yes," she answered daringly.

"Very well. In the morning you will tell Ra-Ta to take you to Ishtar-la. She will be your tutor. Good night now."

Lizla felt blessed and rested. She kept a quiet vigil until dinnertime. She had a lot to think about.

Chapter 4

The Ancient Sacred Coin

The evening came in glowing pinks over the sandy dunes. Shadows of purple fingers ran down through the dark elevations, caressing the ancient slopes where the long-standing shapes of the great pyramids of Giza evoked a past of mystery and wonder.

After the dinner feast—the night of the Nile's blessing festival—Lizla left the quiet Temple grounds, following the gay noise that came from the guest quarters. It was a deep blue sky, pregnant with millions of stars, while the moon was approaching its fullness. Dreamily wandering through the gardens, she passed olive trees and date palms, underneath which the flowerbeds were profuse with roses, jasmines, and lilies. A large verandah surrounded the guest quarters, and a long corridor covered with a heavy mat of vines connected these apartments with the Healing Temple and the Temple of Love.

The Temple of Love was utilized for preparing princesses and nobles for marriage and motherhood. It also functioned to heal the heart wounds and balance the minds of those whose spirits had been broken or bruised by dark emotional experiences. The Healing Temple was another health center dedicated to more physical types of cures than the Temple of Love. Both of them were surrounded by beautiful gardens, whose relaxing and refreshing atmospheres were as much a healing influence as the science that was practiced indoors. The whole complex of the Isis temple was located in a natural oasis, and its lush, vivid greenery provided an uplifting experience for the weary pilgrim who had needed to come through many hours of the desert's incandescent heat.

Here and there among the rose bushes, angel alabaster lamps threw rose, blue, and purple color around the darkening garden. By one of the lamps, by the twisted arm of an old vine, she saw and heard a couple speaking in deep passionate tones. Lizla hid beneath the palm trees as she recognized Psusennes, the lion hunter, whose recent penetrating looks she had found embarrassing. His partner was a young princess of lower rank, Altamira, daughter of Pharaoh's younger brother and one of his concubines. Lizla had seen Altamira before, and although she knew her to be several years her senior, Lizla never felt much respect for her. Her manners were lacking in the serene composure of a real princess, Lizla thought, and her capricious games had hurt Lizla's younger brother and sisters several times. She also was very mean to the servants.

Yet Lizla was puzzled by the way Altamira conducted herself with Psusennes. She was all sweetness and coyness, like a silk and linen doll, lost in his strong arms. Lizla noticed for the first time with admiration his magnificent athletic figure, his muscular shoulders, arms, and legs. He seemed totally absorbed in the playful coquettish smiles of Altamira, who alternated between languid glances and sparkling vivacity. Lizla was puzzled by both. Remembering her newly discovered gifts of psychic perception, she decided to try it on both lovers and understand this new mystery. First she tried it on Psusennes—at the moment in a passionate embrace, pressing his lips against Altamira's, who surrendered with obvious eager desire. His long fingers caressed passionately the slender body of his lover, nude to the waist, while a free flowing skirt covered loosely the well-shaped sun-tanned legs adorned with Persian silk, her sandals embroidered with precious stones. As Lizla tuned into Psusennes, she felt startled. A current of vivid fire came up her womb into her breasts and between her legs. She vaguely remembered the lines of a poem, where the poet described his lover as one "with pomegranate breasts bursting with life and intoxicating power." She looked and touched her own breasts and found they were small and flat compared to Altamira's. A tint of rage mingled with the newfound fire made her take stock of her feelings. Was this a new form of magic?

Altamira's voice was heavy with passion and a slant of jealousy as she complained mildly, "Ah, my lord, thou are a master in the art of Love. By now I thought you had forgotten me for another one, as I'm trapped in this monastery."

Psusennes caressed her lips with his and answered tenderly, "No, my love, you are not trapped here. Your child, our child, shall be born and I'll raise him in my palace. There's no art but magic in the ways of love. Can't you see the miracle of the fruit you bear, and the passion your lips chain to my heart?" Altamira seemed surrounded again, totally lost in her emotions.

As Lizla observed the way Psusennes kissed and caressed her, she felt a mixture of new, inexplicable feelings. There was something regal in his actions, like a lion, like Isis herself. But Altamira's attitude irritated her. How could Psusennes not notice that? Altamira's ways in love were covetous, supplicating, begging, and almost enslaving.

Was that what the magic of love did to women? Lizla felt somehow uneasy, but her proud character rebelled against that. Isis was not like that, but then, she was a goddess. No! Lizla swore to herself, whatever would become of her, woman, queen, or magician, she would never beg for love or tenderness. She would not beg for anything. Ah, but this magic was strong. She had felt it herself. She would have to learn much; she would learn all about it.

Lizla turned away pensively and sat by one of the flowing fountains. The fountains of those temples were illuminated by electricity, a carefully guarded knowledge of the Egyptian priests, as well as other advanced civilizations in the East. Although electricity was considered a magic property and its nature akin to that of the spirits in all living things, its practical applications were exploited to a limited extent. It was used particularly in medicine.

Long copper filaments were set incandescent under very fine crystal rock and glass paste tiles of several colors. The result was a magnificent display of blue, red, and silver streams of water flowing high into the starry night, making light and shadow phantoms of the surrounding date palms. Lizla contemplated the beautiful scene, noting an unusual apprehension cloaking her heart. She could not understand why, but it was an almost forgotten feeling of un-fulfillment that she had not experienced since she left her parents' home. With a sigh, she rose to go back to her room, when on the opposite side of the large fountain she saw another figure seemingly lost in abstract thought. She came close to it as the lights and shadows played tricks with her eyes and would not let her see clearly. Then she was sure. Yes! It was Mikos, the boy she thought lost in her palace days. She ran to his side.

"Mikos!" She greeted him with surprise and excitement. She noticed with grateful surprise that he looked more mature and manly in his approach and posture. His blond curls were shaped gracefully around his newly tanned face. A white toga with the design of the school of medicine covered his tall and athletic body. Also a new look of mature resolution seemed to add strength and dignity to his sparking blue eyes.

"Lizla!" His voice carried almost the same feelings. Then he added seriously, "What are *you* doing here? Are you ill?" Although of Greek birth, he and his older brother Diogenes had been longtime guests of Pharaoh. Mikos was aware of the fact that women rarely got an education like he was getting at the temple.

Lizla felt another pang of pride, the second in that strange evening. "Ill, not so. Do I look it?"

Mikos answered, "No, but I thought, well, I am studying here and you a lady …"

Lizla interrupted him, "A princess. I am a princess. I am also studying here." She held up her chin in an imperious way that Mikos found new and fascinating.

"Well, that is interesting. I'm so glad to see you. A lot of things happened to me. But first tell me about yourself. What are you studying?" Mikos friendly voice was now the old familiar one, although Lizla noticed gleefully that his former shyness was not as pronounced as it had been in the palace. Still, with a majestic mood, she acceded to sit by his side on the tile-covered bench next to the fountain.

She told him about her desert training and her acquaintance with the temple grounds. She carefully omitted the prophecy as well as her whole relationship with Isis as a Mother and special protector. She did relate enthusiastically her experience at the Nile bank with the crocodiles and the healing of the wounded man.

Mikos listened to her story with deep attention. Lizla noticed that his serious intelligence had developed a more mature, deepening tone that pleased her very much. She wondered if he found her grown up likewise. But he was attentive to the facts of her narrative. He had gone through interesting experiences himself, especially one that related to healing.

On one of his school camping trips, he had been taken all the way south to the Nubian border. There, while he was walking by the sparse forest that surrounds the birth of the Nile, he had found an almost dying man. The man had been wounded and left to die, on the border of a quick sand hole. An hour more and he would have gone, but his wounds would not let him move fast enough to make the trip to the safe land, a few yards away. Mikos acted quickly. With the help of his hunting cord and a date palm trunk to which he tied it, he helped the poor man out after a long laborious effort. The man was thankful and mumbled many blessings on his unknown benefactor. But, Mikos could see, it would be almost impossible to heal his wounds. He tried to soothe the man's pain with a vegetable ointment he had learned to make with water and certain leaves. He had to chew the leaves carefully, mentally repeating a healing invocation.

Although he himself was a little more skeptical than the average Egyptian of magic incantations, he tried it anyhow. The man seemed relieved from his pain, but his spirit had been broken. The bandits had killed his teacher and beloved companion, whom he accompanied on an exploring trip. He wanted to die to join his master in the other world, but his teacher had given him quite urgent orders about a certain pouch that contained ancient secrets. It had to be donated to the Isis temple, for it had been in its family for generations and a curse would be upon anyone who lost it or sold it. He thus feared interrupting the fated trip to the Goddess's Temple where the mysterious package belonged.

Intrigued and touched by the continuous supplications of the man, Mikos had promised to fulfill the strange plea. At this, the grateful man laid his head down to rest. He never woke up.

As soon as Mikos returned to camp, he talked to his guide about this strange experience and the impact it had on his vision for the future. He had made up his mind. A solitary meditation had indicated to him what he really was to do. He wanted initiation into the Isis Temple of Medicine! His guide had pondered for a moment. Then, with a meaningful smile he had answered, "Yes, you have my blessings; the Goddess Temple is a great center of healing wisdom and practice. But remember that all you will learn there is neither new nor old. It belongs to eternity. When you come back to your land, you will carry a torch that may be carried on for centuries."

Then his old Egyptian guide and teacher added with a quizzical smile "Are you ready for that challenge?"

The answer had provoked a jolt of pride and excitement in Mikos heart. Surely he was! He could not sleep all night. That very morning, however, he joined a small caravan heading northwest. Soon he found a large boat destined for Memphis.

As Mikos confided his story, Lizla felt a passing sting in her conscience, as she had withheld most of her own story from him. But to her, her destiny was sacred and deeply involved. She decided to keep it a secret. Besides, she was not too sure he would be able to believe it. After all, he was a foreigner.

"Well, don't you want to know what the package contained?" he asked, smiling quizzically. She blushed without knowing exactly why.

"It's not polite to be curious," she retorted, to cover her momentary confusion. For a moment she feared he had read her thoughts! But then she returned to her habitual sweetness. "I would love to hear the rest of your adventure."

"Ah! The adventure hasn't begun yet. By the way, how familiar are you with this Temple?" he asked her.

"Not much. I haven't been here long enough. But I've been exploring it, if that's the word, and I expect to get quite familiar with it very soon." Lizla was surprised by the question.

"Explore, that's the exact word," he answered with unusual force.

She looked at him, really puzzled now: "What do you mean?"

"Let me continue my story," he answered. "After I arrived at the temple, I was surprised to notice that some signs over the big outer murals are quite peculiar." On hearing this, Lizla felt they were touching a subject bordered with the unspeakable mystery.

She said cryptically: "The signs of the Mysteries are only for those who have eyes to see."

Seeing her so serious, Mikos had to restrain himself from laughing. He commented cautiously, "By the Gods, Lizla, you are beginning to sound like one of those mysterious priests."

But she was firm in her position. Ignoring the humor in the remark, she asked calmly, "What signs are those that look so strange to you?"

"Well, they are everywhere. They are the same that appeared in the engraved ancient coin the dying man gave me." He seemed almost irritated with his inability to interpret those.

"Oh, there was an engraved ancient coin in that pouch? Let me see," Lizla said, quite excited.

"I thought curiosity was impolite," he teased her.

"Oh, I was just trying to help you, you know that." But she noticed that he was really pleased with her taking a friendly and open attitude. It was good to feel that way again. Besides, he seemed to be getting into something really interesting.

Mikos searched among the pleats of his tunic and found a small skin leather pouch. It was fastened by a cord of golden silk on the ends of which two crosses of life of pure gold were tightly fastened. Mikos opened it and extracted a round tablet of burnished copper with silver relief on both sides. They brought it close to the nearest lamp and examined it carefully. On one side, there were hieroglyphics with these inscriptions, "To the Glory of Isis, mother of the land whose veil no mortal has yet lifted." These inscriptions, although familiar enough, never failed to touch Lizla's heart. To her the Goddess had always appeared unveiled! There was another symbol they did not recognize. Around the inscription there was a zodiac image. It looked very old. Lizla could not tell, but promised herself to find out when she visited the Astronomy school. The other side had another inscription, this one unfamiliar to both of them. It said: "To the Prince of Peace whose blood will set free the souls of men." There was the picture of a lamb underneath the word *Peace* and another zodiac, totally different from the first one. As Mikos opened the pouch again, this time by the light of the lamp, Lizla noted some writing in the inside of it. She grasped the pouch and turned it inside out. Carefully, they tried to decipher the inscriptions on it. It was a map of the Nile and the City of Memphis marked with a cross. Then, to the left, there was the symbol of Isis and the words, "Great Wall of the sunrise." Beneath it these symbols were marked: the image of a foot, an arrow pointing to the right, the image of two hands, and another foot. All these symbols were enclosed in the eye of a large cross of life that pointed to the north, as a compass star was drawn beside it.

Lizla and Mikos looked at each other in silence. They read each other's thoughts. It was easy: it was a map, but to where? The old man had mentioned the Isis Temple, and the Nile with the cross on the City of Memphis seemed to confirm that, too, since the Temple was close to that city. The Great Wall of the Sunrise, they soon deduced, had to be the eastern wall outside the Temple grounds. It was the first wall to see the face of Ra coming above the horizons every morning. But what about the feet and the hands?

They decided to explore it together. They also decided to keep it a secret. No one should know about this. If they found something good, then there was time to tell. Otherwise they might just make fools of themselves.

They departed each to his and her quarters, promising to meet at sunset the following evening. Everyone else was busy at dinnertime. Lizla promised to get some food for both of them. She simply would inform one of the slaves that she had to study and preferred to have dinner served in her bedroom. Even by the severe Temple rules, a princess had certain privileges.

As she walked into her room, Lizla promised herself to find out three things: the two zodiac dates and the meaning of the Prince of Peace. She had never heard of him before. She might ask Ra-Ta, but for the first time in her life she felt she wanted to withhold this finding from him. After all, she had promised Mikos silence, and if the authorities of the Temple found out, they might take the engraved ancient coin from Mikos and use it for the Temple's museum. Yes, that might happen. She felt that it was important to do that research alone, or with Mikos. Exhausted from such a strange evening, she went to sleep.

Chapter 5

The Pyramid of Light

Ra-Ta had been busy with the schooling preparations for his new disciple. It would take several months for Initiation. Originally a priest of Amon-Ra, God of the sun and dispenser of both human and divine fire, his presence in the Temple of Isis was a temporary one. His mission had been given to him directly by the High Priest of Amon, right after Lizla's birth. The Pharaoh knew about it, so he was welcomed as a guest in the Royal Family as soon as the princess turned twelve. Her mother had requested to be near Lizla a little longer, since she knew that her daughter was destined to strange and high level roles. That was why the normal procedure of match-making and betrothal was spared for her up to the utmost limit: her fourteenth year.

Lizla's natural curiosity and dreamy disposition made her both flexible and original at the same time. For that reason, she never tried to imitate custom and tradition unless she was forced into it. An aura of mystery surrounded the prophecies around her, and so she grew up with the constant premonition of not belonging exactly among her childhood peers. Due to the healthy-hearted and life-loving disposition of the Egyptians in general, her situation was not traumatic by any means, but rather an independent, free-flowing one. She roamed around the palace with numerous siblings and cousins, like most Egyptian children of the high-classes did, thus feeling loved and protected both by their homey families and the benevolent spirits of all things.

Then at the time of her fourteenth midyear, Mother had tried to mingle her with the worldly Babylonian girl, Mizzia, in an attempt to rescue her daughter from a destiny that she feared as both mysterious and frightening. If she could just get her into the regular trend of flirting and merry-making, Mother thought, perhaps she could fall in love with one of the court princes. Thus, in marrying and childbearing perhaps she could be retained at the palace and lead what Mother would call a "normal" life.

But Ra-Ta had intervened in time and found no opposition from Pharaoh. Pharaoh's beloved brother died from wounds received in battle against the Assyrians. After his ascension to the throne, the old king advised the new Pharaoh to see that his niece's education was entrusted to the Priests as soon as they would request it. He knew they kept watch on the stars and received divine guidance through the seers and diviners. The rest was up to the gods. Young Pharaoh had never forgotten that. His older brother's family continued receiving royal treatment at his palace. And he would allow no interference regarding his niece, as he had promised his older brother on his deathbed.

Ra-Ta reflected on all this as he rose up from his morning meditation in the Amon-Ra chapel of Isis Temple. He was not exactly concerned, but keenly aware that the development of a magician was a dangerous task. The fires of the spirit, that awakened could turn a man into a demi-god, were always full of risk and challenge. It was easier perhaps, to set heavy tasks of discipline on a man, already tempered by the rough training in sports and battle. But a woman, especially a princess, was a different story. Lizla had pleasantly surprised him, living up to her Capricorn risings with discipline and determination. Her unusual healing and clairvoyant gifts made the task especially encouraging and rewarding, too. However, this new request that Lizla had received in Meditation about Ishtar-la, really puzzled him. Why, Ishtar-la was the high Priestess of the Love Temple, a powerful, vibrant female, to whom a celibate monk like himself, deeply dedicated to the divine solar fire, avoided cautiously. Now he would probably have to work in cooperation with her. He had to work hard on this, his own way. He decided to retire to three days of fasting and meditation. He was sure his *Ka* would bring an answer to his dilemma.

Lila rose up early in the morning and walked to her favorite bath pool. It was still dark. The clear sky of the desert night would soon release its innumerable stars. Suddenly, beyond the silver streak of light against the eastern horizon, the pristine globe of Ra emerged in orange radiance. Lizla took a dip in the pool, and a few minutes later she got out of it and quickly dried and dressed herself for the morning exercises. She went into the healing temple and joined the others.

The sacred dances could be done with or without music. When she learnt them in the desert, to the sole accompaniment of a reed pipe, she hardly had paid attention to the music. It was necessary to learn the rhythmic exercises that coordinated all body parts into a harmony of progressive speed. There was a deep philosophy behind those movements. But when she had asked Ra-Ta about it, she got no direct answer. Each position combined rhythm, rigorous counting, and skillfully synchronizing several movements of the arms, legs, head, at different levels of speed. The same exercise was done first coordinating all left body parts, then the right ones, and later both together. The whole procedure was repeated three times, each time in increasing speeds. The numbers had special significance, as she correlated them with the knowledge of numbers she acquired in her astrology classes. The numbers 1, 4, 7, and 10 were representations of the controlling forces that act upon the human will. They were always done with the head straight, looking directly in front of one, as if looking for direction.

Ra-Ta had told her to keep paying attention to any suggestion the exercises or the music were giving to her body, as this was "body learning" of a special kind. It was meant to re-establish harmony and beauty to all body parts, but also to learn to accept the voice of intuition directly on the body-cell level, without intellectualizing it. Not even feelings were allowed to interfere with the "body knowledge". That was the reason to learn the exercises, at the beginning, with minimum music. A healer should learn to listen to one's body. It had a wisdom of all its own, and interpretation of the laws of harmony that no theory could comprehend. Then, as telepathy and psychic perception developed, she could learn to "hear" other bodies as well, in order to heal them.

Here at the Temple, the exercises were done with more music. A group of seven players of string and wind instruments did justice to the mysterious melody that alternated between melancholic tones and sharp, almost military, passages. Lizla reflected on this as she joined the small group of students in simple white linen tunics and bare feet who were practicing with her in the music hall of the Isis Temple.

After an hour of dancing, they quietly left hall to enjoy a well-deserved breakfast. Temple students ate silently as they were to commune all physical food with their *Ka*. In thus raising their soul vibrations, both food and mind became spiritualized. A warm, soothing feeling of peace enveloped the small group as they departed to their own respective tasks for the day.

Thankful in her quiet joy, so different from the palace, Lizla came back to her room to await her master's instructions. To her surprise, she found a letter from Ra-Ta on a small silver plate sitting on her table. It contained instructions to spend the next three days getting familiar with the Temple grounds and generally enjoying a short vacation by herself, as Ra-Ta would be involved in a special mission that required total seclusion.

Lizla remembered Mikos and his strange engraved ancient coin. Hoping to find him, she decided to explore the Temple grounds, beginning with the Eastern Great Wall. As she arrived, she was not altogether surprised when she saw Mikos, sitting cross-legged in deep meditation. Lizla stood at a discreet distance of about ten feet. In a few seconds, he turned his head in her direction, showing a triumphant smile.

"You heard me," he said as he rose to greet her.

"Heard you? When?" She pretended to be surprised, as she immediately guessed he must have been practicing some telepathic exercises.

"I was just thinking about you, but you did not seem to receive my message. Perhaps at a subconscious level you heard me, though," he answered rather stubbornly.

"Perhaps you are right," she said. "I've been practicing those exercises myself. But remember, you have to practice in three stages." She stopped talking, wondering if he had been really trained the "official way", as he was a foreigner.

He answered: "Yes, I know: first you practice with the person in front of you. Second, with the same person at a distance, but at an accorded time. And third, with no appointment whatsoever."

"Correct," she sighed, relieved. It looked like their educations were running parallel, at least in these techniques. "Let's practice together now, so we can have a better connection."—She sat on the floor by his side. "By the way, where did you learn to sit that way?"

"Which way?" he asked.

"As you were when I came in, with each foot on the opposite thigh. It must be awfully hard!" She inquired curiously.

"Ah, back in my country, I learned Yoga. This position is called the Lotus pose, because the feet rise up like the petal of a Lotus," Mikos answered as he observed her intently. He could never figure her out. Sometimes she sounded imperious and demanding like a royal princess and other times, she shared his almost childish curiosity about all forms of knowledge. She almost could be Greek; he thought to himself, she has such a thirst for wisdom … He could not deny he really liked her both ways. But a certain competitiveness, which he thought of as mere shyness, kept him for making it too obvious.

"Yoga," answered Lizla, running her delicate fingers over her long shiny hair in a thoughtful gesture of abstract concentration. Then she added with a puzzled smile: "I thought that was a philosophy, sort of a spiritual school."

Mikos drew a breath. He was struck by the splendor of her well-shaped figure and the silky white tunic with golden ornaments shinning in the sun. He felt the hypnotic power of her magnetic eyes, sparkling with fiery interest. The elegance of her dance-like movements as she caressed her long blue-black hair distracted him for a moment from the philosophic discussion.

After a pause, he answered, "Again, back in my country I had an Indian teacher. He was an astrologer too. He was the one who recommended me to come to Egypt; as a matter of fact, he convinced my parents about it. Anyway, this position is called the Lotus position because your feet turn up like the petals of a flower. It also seems to have an effect on certain nervous centers that the Indians called *chakras.*"

Mikos asserted that rather proudly as he saw his young friend seemed to be quite impressed with his short lecture.

"Chakras? What does that word mean?" Lizla asked in a reserved tone as she seemed absorbed in deep concentration.

"I think it means wheels," he answered.

"Wheels! I thought so. So your teacher from India was an initiate. How lucky you are." Then, with a sigh of resignation, she continued: "I learned about those wheels in my desert training. I also saw them in my rebirthing. Perhaps that's why they call that pose a Lotus position. The wheels turn into flower shapes, like an open Lotus, when you meditate correctly. Didn't you know that?" Now it was her turn to give hints and teachings.

"Rebirthing?" He ignored the question. "You did not tell me that you have gone through that! Please tell me more about it." Mikos was astonished again by the many facets he was discovering in his old friend.

Realizing that Mikos's studies were serious and that he had been guided to an initiate, Lizla felt that they were guided by the gods in this conversation. It was all right to talk freely. She briefly described her rebirthing experience to him.

"So you saw me, among clouds of dust, controlling my horses? Or I was having trouble with that? There is a saying in my country: we called it having trouble with your horses when you have a bad temper." He blushed at this confession.

"And do you?" Lizla had always enjoyed teasing him. His fine sensitivity was perhaps his most attractive trait, she thought.

"On occasion." He stood up quite proudly now. "But if you saw that image, then perhaps the message was meant for me. You should have told me about it earlier," he said reproachfully.

"Well, I wasn't sure. You don't spread around things like that lightly." Lizla did feel a little bit of remorse when she saw his face. Yes, he was a good friend, she said to herself. No wonder the gods had put him on her path. "Let's practice now." Lizla was always enthusiastic about learning new things, particularly with a good friend; it was more fun that way.

Mikos resumed the Lotus posture while Lizla sat on her ankles, as she had been trained since childhood. Soon they were practicing telepathy by concentrating on each other. It was an old method they learnt in school: imagine each other's feet to be their own feet, each of their hands to be their own hands and so with arms, legs, body, and mind. A few minutes passed by. Suddenly Lizla felt her friend's voice in her heart. It sounded like her own inner voice, saying: "Do you remember the engraved ancient coin?" She answered silently, "Yes, do you carry it with you?"

Mikos extracted the pouch out of the pleats of his white tunic. He handed it to her, smiling. Lizla took it and examined it carefully. Now, by the daylight, she could see it more clearly. It was made of an old skin—lion skin, it seemed. She wondered how old it was.

Then she opened it, held the engraved ancient coin with her right hand, and turned the pouch inside out.

"There it is," she said, "The map and the message. Let's draw it on the sand."

As they drew the strange symbols on the sand, they were both quite puzzled and remained quietly thoughtful. Their eyes ran from the design on the floor to the great stone wall that faced the eastern horizon.

Suddenly Lizla thought there was a shape of light about four feet from the ground, resting on the wall. As she tried to touch it, the light disappeared. Mikos could not see it, but he had the intuition that something very important was to be revealed. Using a piece of clay as if it were a reed pen, he marked the spot on the wall that Lizla was touching. As soon as he did, the light moved forward, appearing four feet on a northerly direction. Following Lizla's instructions, Mikos marked that spot too. Then he drew a line between the two marks. A perfect square was soon drawn by connecting the line with two vertical lines to the floor.

That was how much they could deduce from the map on the sand. They decided to stop to ask for guidance. After a few minutes of meditation, they both rose to their feet, jumping to the same idea. It worked like a spell. Standing up right between the vertical lines they had drawn from the floor, they both closed their eyes, picturing the Horus symbol, the mystical eye, on their minds' eyes. Then, remembering the instructions on the pouch, while still standing with their eyes closed against the wall, they both stretched their arms to the sides and touched each other's hands. Their hands met in the perfect center of the drawn square! Mikos opened his eyes and again marked that place with his clay instrument. Focusing on that spot and using the golden crosses of life that he found at the end of the streams, they uncovered the mystery of the entrance to the wall!

What they found was a white circle about three inches wide and in the middle a deep red circle. Inside it, in deep relief, they found a cross of life encrusted in the rock. Mikos was surprised to find how easy it was to retrieve the bronze cross from the stone engraving. As he held it in his hand, he noticed that it was a key!

"There it is; let's try it!" Lizla cried impatiently.

"Where?" He was puzzled.

"In the red dot!" Grabbing the key, Lizla rushed to pursue her new idea. She was right: the red dot barely covered the keyhole. With a slight pressure, the key of life entered perfectly into it.

Taking a deep breath, Mikos decided to turn it. What happened next, he would not forget in his entire lifetime. Lizla felt the urge to scream when her friend disappeared beneath a cloud of dust, as he seemed to be moving on a platform going down right beneath his feet. Mikos was surprised speechless, but he managed to get hold of a rail that protected his downward movement. The platform continued downward through what seemed a long journey through a long downward tunnel or corridor. It was very dark. As his eyes got accustomed to the change from the bright sunlight of the desert morning, Mikos began to notice that the walls of the corridor were softened by a diffuse blue-white light. Finally, the platform arrived at the bottom of the tunnel. Mikos looked around, and he felt the urge to step forward. He noticed with alarm that as he did so, the platform initiated a low return back to the surface. Yet his curiosity was great, and in a moment he forgot about the platform. His eyes were absorbed in the strange pyramid of light that shone in front of him, right in the middle of the spacious room where he was standing. It seemed to float on the pristine surface over the marble floor that extended as far as he could see … He approached the gigantic prism with fascination. As he got closer, he felt a deep feeling of peace, strength, and contentment that somehow seemed related to the light but that also focused in his own heart. Then, suddenly, an invisible barrier seemed to stop his forward movement. As he tried to force himself past it, a bright ray of light, crossing through the pyramid, showed a rainbow spectrum wave of light that shook his whole frame as if he had been struck by lightning. Yet he felt no harm. Beyond the invisible barrier that seemed to contain his advancement, the mysterious pyramid stood radiant in its luminous transparency. Mikos was so astonished by the strange scene that he jumped and fell right on his knees, where he remained kneeling for a long time in quiet admiration.

In the meantime, Lizla was watching in expectant fascination at how the platform was slowly coming back up to where she was. She decided to follow her friend. She stepped onto the platform, which gently descended to the bottom. She was astonished at the quiet beauty of the place … it had a soft perfume that reminded her of something. Lizla also saw the pyramid of light, and after her eyes got used to the dark, she tried to approach it. She almost did not see Mikos, who was transfixed and astounded, contemplating it. To his surprise, Lizla went through it and could go inside. But once she went through the barrier of light, even though the pyramid still looked transparent, Mikos could not see Lizla anymore. Lizla advanced timidly inside this inner structure that was suffused by a soft blue light. In the middle of this chamber stood a golden throne. Sitting on it was a very large majestic figure that wore a golden tunic, like a gigantic man with a head like a hawk. She immediately realized she was in front of the god Horus, the son of Isis. She felt intimidated by the incredible majesty of the god. He seemed to smile at her, but overwhelmed with awe and a bit of fear, she bowed to the floor.

The god's voice had a strong tone that was imperious and harmonious at the same time: "Daughter of the light; what do you seek?"

"I am seeking the meaning of this prophecy and the path shown by the engraved ancient coin," Lizla said cautiously. Then, she felt impelled to continue: "And.… and I really don't know. Because these sweet but terrifying experiences keep coming to me, and I feel compelled to keep seeking." She felt rather silly and confused; who was the owner of the voice anyhow? Could she ask him? Again, she mustered courage: "Who are you?"

The god's voice was sonorous, filling the space and rather encouraging, uplifting the heart. It said warmly: "I am Horus." And his name rippled out into the silence. At least, that is what Lizla thought, because she felt a deep need to hear it again and again.

"Horus, Horus," she chanted, almost inaudibly. By then, they pyramid of light had changed to a deep red wave of light that vibrated like a gigantic heart. Lizla was mesmerized by the spectacle, and she saw the flash of the tiny blue light that appeared in the middle of the red pulsating light. Lizla had the impression that for an instant, the tiny blue pearl grew up into a huge eye that disappeared into the light almost immediately. Lizla closed her eyes to test their vision. When she opened them, she was surprised again. The pyramid had changed again to the soft quiet blue. The silence was deep. Suddenly she felt a hand touching her left shoulder. Lizla shouted with terror and fell to the floor, fainting.

"Lizla, Lizla are you all right?" Mikos's alarmed voice woke her up as she felt him shaking her arms. Slowly, she opened her eyes. The pyramid had disappeared.

"What happened?" She asked with a mixture of confusion and anxiety that made Mikos even more worried.

"What happened?" Mikos exclaimed. "You tell me! You disappeared inside the blue … whatever it was … and then there was a big flash of light that almost blinded me! And now here you are—we are!—inside this old tomb or something!" He looked around with apprehension.

"Tomb? No, it was, it is the pyramid, underground. Don't you remember?" Lizla fumbled with her words to answer.

"Remember? What? I don't know anything except that we came down here; I don't know how … how do you know it is not a tomb anyhow?" He retorted.

"I have a feeling," she replied absentmindedly, looking around herself for orientation.

"Your feelings have gotten us into mighty trouble. Here we are, trapped alive in this tomb … I don't know how we came in, so how are we going to get out?" Mikos was exasperated. But Lizla could hardly concentrate on his tirade. She was still under the glow of her incredible experience, when the blue light had turned red. Like a short-lived fire.

"Relax!" She replied. "Our stars have not decried for us to be in trapped in a tomb at this age, remember?"

"Remember ..." the Greek boy answered. "Yes I do! That we are late for the astrology class and the breakfast. I am sure we've missed both already." Mikos could hardly contain his fear and frustration.

"Astrology! Yes! Oh, I know I will find a way," she mused absent-mindedly as she got up and headed for the still platform that had brought them down.

"Come here!" she called.

"Oh! Not again," Mikos grumbled, but for want of a better solution he followed her to the platform, which soon afterwards ascended slowly like a floating magic carpet. When it seemed that their heads were going to crash against the ceiling, it opened up against the brightness of the desert sun, which created a flood of light over the small platform. In a few seconds, they stepped outside.

Mikos cried with relief as he saw in the distance the small line forming out of the dining area. Breakfast was a still going on! Waving a quick goodbye, Mikos ran to join the food line. Lizla, feeling still puzzled and awed, followed him, walking dreamingly at a very slow pace. She needed to wash up before breakfast. Besides, she could order it to her room. She needed a few minutes alone.

Mikos sat alone at the breakfast table. He did feel his honey cakes had a very strange taste this morning. Suddenly he felt very lonely. He remembered how far and distant, long ago in his Greek native homeland, ripe figs and grapes would have accompanied the warm goat's milk that his mother always had ready for him. It was not usual for him to feel homesick. But Lizla puzzled him beyond measure. She was obviously not an ordinary girl, but in addition, somehow Mikos felt a curious mixture of feelings about her. She was beautiful, dignified like a princess, and perhaps too much like a princess. But besides that, she seemed to embody that annoying Egyptian character. So much on the mystical side! Not that he was not interested in mysticism himself; he was so, very much. But for him, it was more a subject of experiment or study. But these Orientals, he thought to himself, particularly Lizla, they seemed altogether at home in this strange world of mysteries! Like she disappeared inside his vision—or was it a common vision? And what does it mean? And why was he withheld from entering into it? And she had seemed lost in thought, but not in feeling! What kind of lightning underground had shocked her like that? It had taken him a long time to wake her up. If it had been up to him, he would have run for dear life. But no, she fell asleep so peacefully or so it seemed! What did she see? How come a terrifying experience like that seemed to have filled her with such a strange composure?

"I will never understand these people!" he mumbled to himself. He did not realize he had voiced his last comment aloud.

Soon he heard a familiar voice echo his sentiment: "I'd say so." Annouk-Aimee was sadly smiling.

"What are you doing here?" He recognized his sister, whom he thought was stationed in the royal court as one of the Queen's attendants.

"I came for study and healing," his sister answered.

"Healing from what? Are you in trouble or ill? Please, by Jove, please tell me all about it!"

"Princess Lillie and Diogenes … well, they had a fight. And I barely escaped from her anger." Annouk-Aimee started timidly. Diogenes was their older brother.

"She took it out on you? How come, I say … now these people!" Mikos was getting seriously upset now.

"No, they were not at fault." Annouk-Aimee could hardly raise her eyes from her rabbit skin sandals with which she was creating a small mound of sand around her brother's chair. Mikos smiled. Annouk-Aimee was the younger sister in the family. Always self-willed and impulsive; it wasn't a new experience for Mikos to have to come to her rescue.

"Tell me what happened. What did you do? I promise I won't tell mother. I'll try to help you, but you have to follow my advice. Not like the last time."

"Mikos, oh, Mikos," she cried anxiously, burying her head in his brother's arms.

"Oh, no, let's get out of here." Mikos took her by the hand and led her into the long corridor lined with tall and wide palm trees that led to the main fountain that divided the Temple of Isis's main gardens from the entrance to the Temple of Love.

The soft rustling palm leaves above their heads were the only sound that accompanied Annouk-Aimee's sobbing. Mikos kept on wondering what the stars had in store for him that morning. Women's troubles kept pouring onto him.

Annouk-Aimee had to gather all her strength to break the news to her brother: "I think I'm pregnant."

"What!" Mikos's cry startled her even more. "How on earth did this happen? All these soft-spoken Egyptians, with their courteous manners! I told you they are only trouble. Liars and traitors, all of them. How could you have trusted any one of them? You know what mother would have thought about this? She would have called you a …" Mikos stopped himself, seeing that his sister came to pieces on the floor, her long blonde hair mixing with the leaves that lay on the sandy ground. Looking at his sister, fragile, scared and desolate, Mikos's heart softened.

"Who was it? Tell me! I'll kill him! And Diogenes, does he know about this? What did he say? How come he did not contact me? Does mother know about this?"

Annouk-Aimee sat on the floor. Her eyes were full of tears. An infinite sadness covered her face at the mention of so many loved one's names who would be affected by her problem.

"It was an Assyrian; he tricked me. That is why I was sent to the Temple of Love—to be healed and to learn, I guess," she added softly. "He is no longer alive; Diogenes had him killed. Or rather she did, Princess Lillie. Diogenes wanted to face him, to kill him himself, but Lillie got him quietly poisoned. I think that's why they were fighting: over something about royal court politics. Later, I remember Diogenes saying something about feeling overpowered, or how did he put it, manipulated by her. Anyhow, she did not want a scandal."

But now Mikos was concerned about something else. Forgetting for a moment about his sister's plight he asked her, "What kind of political problems? Why did he feel manipulated by her? Is Diogenes in danger too? Do you know?"

Annouk-Aimee sighed with relief at the opportunity to change the subject. "I don't know, but Diogenes had made friends with a few Assyrians and a very mysterious Persian. Lillie was very impatient with those friendships. She felt they were not reliable. It also seems that she knew something else that made her very uneasy about her lover's association with these people".

Mikos embraced his sister and gave her a soft kiss on the forehead. "I think you've had enough talk for now. Go to your room and keep quiet. If you need anything, you know where to find me. Please make sure Mother doesn't know anything about this."

Chapter 6

The Astrology Lesson

Lizla was feeling uncomfortable sitting on her exalted cushion in the upper balcony. Being a princess had some privileges. Coming late to class without being scolded was one of them, because she could come in quietly through the backstage stairs into the balcony. There she found her seat in the dark, opened her perfumed book chest and unwrapped the silver cords that protected her papyrus notebook.

The old Indian sage did not seem to notice her late arrival. That made her feel relieved but somehow frustrated at the same time. She liked to be noticed. Also, she worried: had she missed something important? She noticed that already, in the lower levels, the other students seemed rapt in attention. Swami Suryananda was pointing to a chart hanging on the wall on the back of the stage. On it he had painted the planetary setup for the day and was explaining the current events. Lizla realized with regret that probably she had missed the introductory *mantras*, those mysterious Indian prayers that always fascinated her when she arrived on time. She pondered that with a mixture of admiration and apprehension. What would the Egyptian gods think about those foreign prayers? On the other hand, she had been told that Suryananda meant the "Bliss of the sun". The sun was Ra, the chief god among the Egyptians. She also had been told, and she had even seen, the Indian master beautifully performing his morning ablutions by the large pool in the Temple of Ra, and then humbly prostrated himself as the sun god arose in the eastern horizon.

As if catching up with her thoughts, Suryananda raised his eyes towards the upper balcony. His face lit up with a fleeting smile as he perceived in the dark his royal disciple. Then promptly he went back to the charts explanation.

"An eclipse will occur today at noontime as the planet Ketu crosses over the sun."

He paused, as he knew the effect that even a moment of obscuration of the divine protector of Egypt would have over his students.

"But the sun will triumph over Ketu, and come out of the shadows about three hours later." Ignoring the anxious looks from the auditorium, he continued: "Now let us look at the significance that has been pointed to by these events. On the national scene, the eclipse could indicate a temporary time of defeat for your forces in Aswan. The life of the Pharaoh may be endangered …"

A muffled cry of terror was suffocated in the throats of his polished and attentive listeners.

"But he will survive, and so will most of his forces," Suryananda concluded reassuringly.

Lizla could not help admiring again the majestic presence of the Indian master with his long matted hair flying over the stage as he displayed a sign of triumph while he described Ra's triumphal passage over the disturbing Ketu.

"The messages of the heavens are not meant only to predict events outside, but also to enlighten the roads of knowledge into our own souls," the sage continued. "Ketu, the dervish, represents wisdom, mystery, and occult knowledge—the kind of knowledge you are acquiring today. The sun also represents the soul, and life itself in its most brilliant manifestation. Its presence reveals the glories of the sky and land, flowers and stocks, food, play, drink, pleasure, and all the delights that our beloved father lavishes us with."

Swami wasn't a monk, but he was a Brahmin, a dedicated Indian scholar. Lizla noticed that he never lost an opportunity to remind his privileged audience about the trappings of a life of luxury.

Swami Suryananda continued, "Today the sun will pass through a period of quiet darkening, conceding to the white gods of quiet meditation, the center stage. It is a special opportunity for all of us. There, in the quiet power of our inner silence, we can pray for the protection of the king and the future of your beloved land."

And again he turned his burning eyes to the whole royal audience and other members of the court, who together with the gifted Temple priests, constituted his attentive class. His manners where quite independent and almost fearless, as he quietly withdrew behind the hanging wall chart.

The musicians arranged the center stage to prepare for the morning chant.

An eclipse, Lizla thought, war and defeat ... trouble in the South!

The students murmured, "And this Indian Master expects us to go into quiet meditation? Does he not know any fear? Maybe a traveling monk has lost all feeling of home and country. How does he dare to speak like this to our princes and princesses?"

The musicians started the soothing rhythm created by lyres and vinas and a mysterious Indian drum called "tabla", which had almost a hypnotic effect on Lizla's consciousness. The chant was done in Sanskrit, a language that Lizla wanted very much to learn, because she was so interested in Vedic astrology. She made a note to ask Ra-Ta about that after he finished his mysterious isolation.

The leading chanters started with a hymn to the sun, which started on slow tones deep in reverent feelings, which Lizla found strangely reassuring in spite of the foreign language. The priests of the sun, whether Indian or Egyptian, were always her teachers, she thought as the beloved face of Ra-Ta, her master and Egyptian guru, passed before her inner eyes.

In many ways, Ra-Ta, with his impeccable Egyptians manners, was very different from the flamboyant Indian master. But a fire in their eyes, she recognized, came in both cases from Ra himself. Maybe that was why they were both destined to be preceptors of kings and princes. Who could tell the ways of heaven?

"Ah!" she thought. "But the ways of heaven are what they try to interpret, aren't they? Not for me," she told herself. "I'd rather help people. At least then I know what I'm doing."

Lizla joined fervently in the religious chant. They came right up to fever pitch after a slow crescendo. The sun was high on the horizon, but it was still pitch black inside the Hall of Stars. Only the tiny butter lamps and the glow of the incense sticks were visible. But Lizla did not see them any longer, as she was submerged into the sweetness of the chant with its velvety softness. It numbed her senses and caressed her mind into a state of total stillness.

She felt she was going into deep meditation when all of a sudden a vivid scene appeared in her mind's eye. She was a standing by a well, fetching a pail of water and drinking in the Sun's caresses of the early morning. All of the sudden, a gigantic rider on a colossal black horse approached from the southwestern horizon. He galloped towards her at full speed and seemed closer and closer by the minute. In her vision, Lizla stood up, her heart beating furiously with a mixture of fear and excitement. Friend or foe? Was she safe? Somehow she felt she knew him, but before he could get close enough so she could see his face, the chimes pronouncing the end of the chant sounded, announcing the opening of the huge doors of the Hall of Stars, and the glorious glow of the desert sunlight interrupted her dream.

Almost irritated, Lizla stood up, put her papyrus in order, and followed the line of students to the dining hall where refreshments were being served.

"Eat lightly, but well. If possible, avoid lunch meals. It is no good to eat heavily at eclipse time. You may want to keep a light stomach for the noonday meditation. Today it can be especially powerful."

Those where the parting instructions from the swami's secretary as they abandoned the Hall of Stars Auditorium.

Chapter 7

The Solar Eclipse

Lizla sat quietly in her meditation room after the light early lunch that was allowed during the eclipse. Following the quiet breathing exercises that had the power to bring her into the inner chambers of her soul, she thought of Ketu. Swami had told them a strange story about Ketu. It was an old Indian legend. It went like this:

Many hundreds of years ago, the gods and the demons had a big fight for the supremacy of the three worlds. The gods were not yet immortal at that time, but they were wholly *satvic* or pure souls that were always championing the ways of heaven. The demons were rebellious souls (the Indians called them *Rakshakas*). They were both mischievous and irresponsible. They could be fierce in battle, but cruel in victory with their enemies as well as with innocent or weak bystanders. They liked to live in forests. Lizla wondered how that could be so bad, because here in the desert, trees were scarce and deeply revered. But the legend said those demons could attack innocent people who walked through the woods, particularly children. The worst of them ate young children, but they all had the tendency to scare them away from their parents and terrify them with noises and ghostly shadows.

In that fight, the Lord of the Word, Vishnu, was the Hindu sustainer of the universe. He was the upholder of Dharma or righteousness. Dharma was the equivalent of "*ma'at*"—the Egyptian word for universal order. At this point in the story Lizla recalled her previous teachings: Yes, the heavens and the earth were supported by ma'at and Amon-Ra shined among them. But Amon-Ra was not on that Indian story.

The God of Love, another title for Vishnu, declared that the struggle would be decided by a single contest. Both gods and demons would churn the ocean of milk that was in a celestial container that rotated around a central pole that Vishnu was holding. Vishnu himself held the central pole, acting as the final and supreme arbiter of the contest.

The gods and the demons churned the ocean of milk furiously, until it became solid like butter. Just before the ocean solidified, a beautifully dressed Goddess covered with jewels, emerged from it. Behind her was the God of Medicine, carrying with him the nectar of immortality, which the Indians called Amrit. Lizla thought about Isis and her power as a healer. She wondered if the Goddess arising from the ocean of milk was the Indian version of Isis. She had asked Suryananda about this, but Suryananda declined to comment and answered cryptically: "We call her Lakshmi, the Goddess of Abundance."

After the gods and demons jumped out of the now solid ocean, they were asked to form a line to drink from the Amrit that the God of Medicine was distributing. The arrangement had been made between Vishnu and the gods that the gods would be first in the line, to ensure they would become immortal, while Vishnu would make sure that the demons did not enter the line. The planets were considered gods, so they also joined the line. But a very clever demon called Rahu sneaked into the line among the gods. Suddenly the Sun and the Moon, which are the brightest among the planets, noticed the intrusion and told Vishnu about it. The God Vishnu was very angry at the demon and, picking up his sword, he cut the demon in two.

Unfortunately, the demon Rahu had already drunk of the nectar, so it did not die but instead, it split in two. The head portion became Rahu and the tail portion became Ketu. The rest of the strange legend related how Ketu drank with both victory and confusion (a common state of mind for most demons) fell over the roof of one of the houses over which he was jumping around, in his frenzied dancing. As he fell down from the roof, he landed in a flowerpot owned by a very pious Brahmin wife. Ketu blessed the plant that provided him with a refuge from the fury of Vishnu. That year the plant yielded its most beautiful flowers. The pious woman blessed the flowerpot and its new inhabitant grew into a sage in his next lifetime. Thus Ketu became the symbol of the preservation of knowledge and wisdom and the protector of sages and scholars. The legend ended with both Ketu and Rahu making a lifelong vow to punish the sun and the moon for having denounced them to Vishnu. They persecuted the sun and the moon all the time and, true to their demonic nature, when they encountered them, they ate them. When Rahu or Ketu devoured either the Sun or the Moon, an eclipse was formed. Rahu and Ketu were the symbolic names of the North and South nodes of the Moon. Their demonic nature thus explained the presence of eclipses, as well as the disruptive influence they had in the life of people. For in the areas where their presence was found in human astrological charts, and in their cycles of life as well as in planetary aspects, both Rahu and Ketu, but specially Ketu, tended to create disruptive effects. Lizla thought about all of this, as she continued the breathing exercises that preceded the afternoon meditation.

The whole Temple had been closed and dedicated to inner practices due to the eclipse. It was an eerie feeling, but after some quiet chanting Lizla experienced a very deep peace. This time, however, the feeling of peace was not accompanied with contentment and trust, as she was accustomed in her orderly and well protected life. In its place, a heavy feeling was over her shoulders, and suddenly her third eye opened like a window where clear images were displayed, followed by periods of foggy anxiety.

She saw a multitude of boats approaching the armies that her uncle Ramses X was leading. And they were the "sea people" swarming over the Delta of the Nile. Unfortunately they were killing men and burning and sacking villages. They took the women alive and killed soldiers and older people. Lizla's heart was pumping fast with anxiety. She saw her uncle fighting valiantly, but eventually the Egyptians retreated into the Tanis palace. She also saw the old priests at Thebes, celebrating a victory secretly outside the temple. She saw particularly a young man called Iutus, who had a party at the home of a Libyan general. Earlier in the afternoon, they had had another meeting in the outskirts of the Amon-Ra Temple.

Lizla did not want to see anymore. She wondered if Ketu was playing tricks on her mind. Demons did that sometimes. But at that moment she was interrupted by a sudden vision of her mentor, Ra-Ta.

He said, "Lizla, please remember that there is a full moon over your natal rising sign—where Ketu is situated in your chart-and for that reason you are having these visions. They are a gift from the gods, showing you some signs of things to come. Pray for Isis's protection, Ketu is with you, as he is blessed by your guru planet that aspects it. Never forget that."

Lizla quietly initiated the Isis invocation, and the images disappeared. Soon the familiar rosy glow covered her heart as she felt the soft pressure of a gentle hand on her eyebrows. She quickly fell asleep.

Chapter 8

Rumors of War

Three hours passed. Suddenly the trumpets that heralded the triumph of the Sun-Ra out of the shadows woke her up. Quietly, she rose and went outside, walking dreamingly by the man-made lake that flanked the palace on the westerly garden. Lizla had spent many an afternoon listening to Ra-Ta's lectures and following him in the chanting and dancing exercises that celebrated the sun's departure in glorious colors on the western horizon.

This time she was alone, or so she thought. Absentmindedly, she sat by a marble bench beneath a palm tree whose melodic palm leaves offered a soothing rhythm for her stressed nerves. The shade of the palm tree and its quiet reflection on the water made her almost forget all the strange visions, when she overheard two familiar voices and a strange one, reaching her ears almost against her will.

Unaware of her quiet presence, sitting quietly facing the lake, the voices were commenting on the events of the week. The first voice she recognized was that of Diogenes; the second was Aunt Lillie. There was another one that fascinated her. It had a melodious Persian accent and spoke in passionate tones. Lizla decided not to reveal her presence and hiding behind a big palm tree, kept quiet and listened.

"The sea peoples are formidable sailors, but they have no chariots or land. Even their horses do not compare with ours," Diogenes was saying.

"What do they want with us?" Lillie inquired.

Lizla was surprised to hear a tone of fear in her admired beautiful aunt. She had always seen her as the leading royal figure at many parties, full of confident smiles, with her exquisite perfumed aura and blinding golden jewelry.

"They are nomads," the Persian was saying. "They envy the grandeur, riches, power, and stability of your Egyptian kingdom."

"But you cannot grow kingdoms on boats." Diogenes's mind was as clear as his Greek accent, Lizla thought to herself, remembering her own friend Mikos, Diogenes's brother.

"No, but you can steal its riches and run—if you have that kind of tradition," the Persian added gravely. "It is not easy to be nomads. They do not have our solid habits and possessions. They worship freedom and would feel suffocated in a city, palace, or temple."

The Persian voice had an almost poetic tone that Lizla found most intriguing. Still, the argument irritated her.

"Too free to build and harvest, but no qualms about stealing the fruits of other's labor and stability?" Lizla reflected with agitation. There was no *ma'at* in that argument. She hoped Aunt Lillie would defend the same ideals. But she was disappointed to realize that Aunt Lillie was no philosopher.

"What can we do to stop them?" Lillie inquired anxiously.

"We need to find strong allies, like the Libyans," suggested the Persian voice.

"But they are our traditional enemies," ventured Lillie. She did not want to hear more. She missed her late husband. He had been a strong warrior and had lost his life defending Lizla's father, the late Ramses IX, whom both princesses still adored.

Lillie ran to the palace, saying she had official duties to attend to. The Persian, whom Lizla learned was called Ramee, continued.

"I hope I did not offend the Princess. I assure you that was never my intention."

Diogenes answered, "It was not you; it was her memories. Her husband died in a furious fight with the Libyan, in the wars that also killed the last Pharaoh."

Ramee was very sorry after this explanation. "Now she probably hates me. How insensitive of me," he mused sadly.

"Don't worry," his friend advised. "She is a mature, although still young, lady and well trained in the way of court and politics. Actually, I find her rather intelligent for a woman. Her early widowhood and the tragedies in her family have made her more aware than other women. She keeps informed and is objective. She also loves the poetry of your countrymen and the beauty of the Persian tapestries. You should see her palace …" He held himself, as he was about to be indiscreet about their private relationship. Ramee smiled softly and changed the subject.

"So what do you actually know about the sea peoples' movement?" Ramee inquired. "I heard they were keeping spies in the Thebes temples."

Diogenes put his hand abruptly over the young Persian's mouth.

"Be careful, my friend. This garden has ears sometimes. Do you like hunting? Meet me tomorrow at sunrise by the Eastern Portal."

With that, the friends parted.

Lizla got up and went to her room. She found a note from Mikos. He apologized for being sharp with her early in the morning. He was startled by the events but appreciated her friendliness and her company very much. He asked for forgiveness.

"There is nothing to forgive," Lizla answered mentally. Mikos's outburst was the least of her problems. She also wanted to meet him. She had a million questions on her mind and his refined logic and sharp mind was always a welcome relief to her psychic sensitivity and fiery imagination.

She sent an answer back, that she would like to meet him after dinner by the main fountain. Lizla changed clothes, put a new wax cone with lotus perfume on her long hair, and after washing her feet, she put on a new pair of silk sandals. They were from Persia, she remembered. The merchant had told her so at the last caravan fair where she purchased them. She wondered what Persia looked like. The sandals were white with golden cords and were embroidered with pearls. She imagined a pair of hands with pearly rings and a soft voice with moon tones of pearl rings like the young man she had heard but not seen that strange afternoon. Obviously, Ketu was overcome by the sun, but left behind his trail of mysteries. And those mysteries had been so consistent in the last three months. Lizla could hardly remember her "normal" life at the palace in Tanis with her younger brothers and sisters. She wondered how Mother was. Perhaps it was time to visit home. She hoped her family would not feel affected by the political intrigues she was hearing about and envisioning.

After dinner, the soft procession of lute and papyrus vines celebrated the triumph of the sun over Ketu. And the sky also celebrated Ra's victory with passion, Lizla thought, as she contemplated the glorious tones of golden and crimson clouds on the western horizon.

Mikos arrived and could not help admiring her fine features, made even more beautiful by the golden glow of the sunset on her skin and her bright white gown.

He called her name softly, "Lizla."

Lizla smiled dreamily as she pointed to a seat next to her on the border of the magnificent fountains.

"What an incredible day, wasn't it?" Lizla started, and she wondered aloud if the eclipse, with its influence of Ketu over the sun, had anything to do with their experience underground earlier in the morning.

"Who knows? Perhaps," mused Mikos. "It was surely a day full of mysteries, and I am not sure I can get adjusted to all this heavy mysticism."

"It is not so usual for me either," Lizla said, while she thought inwardly: "There is nothing 'heavy' about mysticism,"

But Mikos interrupted, “But you Egyptians are surrounded by Gods and mysteries. This is what I came to learn, but sometimes it is too much.”

Lizla smiled. Mikos did have a need to keep things organized in his mind and resisted the ways of the imagination. She did not fully understand why.

“If this is what you came to find, you should be happy. It is not so common. It is a blessing. Truly, our traditions have many gods and legends. But actual experience is a blessing. We should be grateful to the gifts of heaven.” Lizla frowned a bit, after she considered her own advice.

Mikos laughed softly. “Oh Lizla, that is not what I mean, but the way you seem to go in and out of it, like nothing happened.” Mikos looked at her quizzically.

“In and out of what? Life has many faces. I don’t think we are in and out of anything, just experiencing many things … Some of them are easier to explain, truly, but some things that are easy to explain are not always blessings.” A cloud of fear and irony accompanied her last words.

Mikos thought about his encounter with his younger sister and agreed seriously. Sitting close to her, he contemplated quietly the last rays of the sun sinking behind the horizon.

Mikos decided to confide in Lizla about his concerns regarding his younger sister. He quickly related the encounter in the morning. Lizla was quiet during the difficult sharing and tried to listen without looking at him directly. She averted his gaze by looking to the floor.

Then she said softly, “Well, the same thing happened to my friend Mizzia, but her aunt helped her. What did you say to your sister? How did she take it? Is she all right?”

“She was crying like a baby. I tried to scold her, but she finally melted me down,” he said with a sigh of shame for having lost his adamant older brother posture. Lizla was puzzled at first and then grew increasingly angry at him.

"You tried to scold her when she came running to you in tears? She is alone, in trouble, in a foreign country, stationed in a foreign court! How could you be so cruel? She needs you."

"Well, she always gets into trouble. She always got into trouble even as a little child. She is the youngest of ten brothers and sisters. Her older sister is twelve years her senior, is married to a Greek general, and has three children. Annouk was always the baby of the family and she did what she pleased, always disobeying. I remember she got sick at the age of six by eating a whole bowl of green grapes, and the day she marched an entire group of chickens on our mother's clothes when Mother was preparing for a big feast. I was hoping some day she would grow up, but then, when she does, she gets into more trouble."

Lizla smiled at the thought of the mischievous child. She did not look like a naughty child now. Lizla knew Annouk-Aimee as the preceptor of Princess Lillie's growing children. She was teaching them to read and write the Greek language. She seemed an intelligent and dedicated teacher. Lizla loved languages and had wanted to ask her for Greek lessons.

She answered Mikos, "Well, maybe she was used to all this attention at home and felt alone in an Egyptian palace. You know, we are different. Our modes and our beliefs in ma'at and decorum are often misunderstood as coldness." Lizla added, "Also, Mizzia is taking care of the palace children, and she loves to tell elaborate romantic stories. She caught my imagination for a while too. She must have caught Annouk-Aimee up in her tales." Then she had an idea: "I always loved to learn new languages, and Greek is important for learning and traveling. Do you think Annouk-Aimee would teach me? Maybe this way she could find a quieter friend."

Mikos looked at her with surprise and admiration. "Annouk-Aimee and you? I just can't picture it. You two are so different." He laughed softly and shook his head.

Lizla was not easily deterred. "Well, women bond easier than men, so my mother used to say. Mizzia is very different from me, too, and we were good friends."

"Yes, and Ra-Ta did not like it, you said," Mikos retorted.

"Well, my master was preparing me for initiation. But I would like to get to know your sister better."

Mikos reflected. "Maybe it could work. She may need the gentle advice of a young intelligent woman, and she would be proud to befriend a royal princess." He decided to agree, but he added pleasantly, "Yes, it could work, but I have a favor to ask you. Can you please teach her to meditate? That could help her to mature a little faster, perhaps."

Lizla laughed softly. "Here you are, judging the poor girl again. Just leave it to me. I'll see what I can do." She became pensive.

Mikos felt a little remorseful, but that made him defensive."Well, in my country we care for our women and their honor … "He started.

"Ready to kill for it, like your brother Diogenes?" Lizla felt a bit defiant now. "What honor is it to commit murder? You said the girl was playful. How do you know they were not just playing love games and he then….? Because Assyrians are not mild people. And, by the way, most peoples are not as 'mental' as the Greeks often are!" Lizla was surprised at her own irritable reaction. She was tired and overwhelmed with all the powerful experiences. She made an effort to soften up and continued with her habitual comforting tone.

"I did not mean to put your people down. I admire your bright minds and clever speaking qualities, but sometimes I notice you tend to live in your thoughts a lot. That makes sudden judgments, good and bad, black and white." Lizla sighed and started playing with the strands of her jet-black long hair. Mikos could not help smiling at the way that the chirping streams of the fountain, with its multiple colors, were reflecting on her hair and diamond necklace, creating a splendid effect.

"We also have an eye for beauty," Mikos ventured timidly, as he admired her once more.

In the twilight, Lizla hoped her blushing would not show much, as she felt her cheeks suddenly burning.

"Speaking of the Assyrians," she continued, "Aunt Lillie's reaction to getting Annouk Aimee's lover killed would tell you something about how much we care for our women's honor, too. Particularly, we honor guests we host in our homes."

Mikos reflected aloud, "Yes, and Diogenes told me about it this afternoon. It could bring political problems for her. The Assyrians have strong connections in the palace and especially further south in the Thebes temples. But don't worry. From what I heard of Diogenes's friends, they would not appreciate the misconduct of one of them in the royal court of the Pharaoh's sister. They might have killed him themselves, but you are right, now she must be careful, as we all ought to be."

It was Lizla's turn to share her own experiences and concerns about the political situation. "What do you know about the Hittites and the sea people?"

"Well, how do you know about this?"

Lizla related the conversations she had overheard by that very fountain when she came to refresh herself after the afternoon meditation. Mikos confided that he had shared dinner with his brother Diogenes that same evening and Diogenes had confirmed that the same issues were concerning many people in the palace.

"Well, I don't know much about the Hittites except that by both our standards and yours, you would not call them truly civilized," Mikos said with a sudden surge of pride.

"How come?" Lizla wanted to know, but Mikos refused to describe to her the wild stories he had heard about their religion or their cruelty in battle and with prisoners.

"I don't think a lady of your stature should be hearing these things. Believe me, if you ever have a Hittite invasion; make sure that you and your ladies are hidden underground safely. You also do not want your children to fall in their hands. They make human sacrifices with children, I am sorry to say."

Mikos did not want to scare his delicate friend with these gruesome tales, but he felt he needed to protect her somehow.

"Well, you do tend to protect your women," Lizla thought to herself as she smiled shyly. She stopped herself in the middle of her own thought as she realized she had thought "your women." Avoiding his admiring gaze again, she persisted: "What about the sea people?"

"Oh, those are nomads floating on water." Mikos laughed at his own improvised definition. "They are very good sailors, and I understand that in a sea battle they are formidable warriors. However, they do not have a developed civilization like yours. They envy your granaries and your riches. So they act often like pirates. They only land to steal and replenish their boats. They speak the most ambitious talk about landing and conquering, but they have not been able to prevail over your mighty armies."

"What about women and children?" asked Lizla with a tone of anxiety.

Mikos smiled and decided to tease her about it. "They are mainly after supplies, but if they see a very beautiful woman, well, they are men."

This time, Lizla truly blushed and announced she was a bit tired and wished him goodnight.

Lizla went back to her room and felt a bit dizzy. So many things had happened in a few days. She was afraid of going to sleep for fear of having a bad dream, but the moment she reclined in her bed she fell deeply asleep. She dreamt that Ra-Ta was turning in his bed with anxiety, which puzzled her. Ra-Ta had always been such an example of composure and almost hermetic equipoise. But now she heard him crying out, "No, no, who are you?" She also saw that the stranger that was hiding behind the curtains of his bed came out of the shadows and said menacingly, "You have to go to Thebes. The high priests are dealing with the Assyrians. We know you have influence at the palace. Leave right now. We have a palanquin waiting for you." Ra-Ta fixed his eyes on the stranger, which made the young man hesitate, and with a quick maneuver, Ra-Ta took the youth's dagger out of his trembling hand. This time, Ra-Ta threatened the stranger to speak: "I said who are you? How did you get in here? Who sent you?"

"I am Narum, of Nubian ancestry. My mother is Egyptian and works at the palace. My father was killed by the priests of Amon-Ra in Thebes. I swore to avenge his death, but my mother warned me against it. She said that Ra protects his children. But I can see now that you are a holy man. And I was brought up to revere your kind. Still, I need to avenge my father."

Ra-Ta felt compassion for the young man and decided to help him out. "Your name is Narum. That is not an Egyptian name. Were you named after your father?" The young man's wild eyes had calmed down a bit by now.

"Yes, he was a general in the Nubian army, but he told me that the Egyptians and the Nubians had a peace treaty dating from the great Pharaoh."

Ra-Ta was pensive. "That is true. For close to five generations there has been peace between the two lands. You said your father was assassinated by an Egyptian priest. Who told you that?"

The young Nubian was afraid to speak. "If I tell you, my mother may be in danger. You can kill me, but I won't speak."

Ra-Ta put a reassuring arm on the distressed youth's shoulder. "I am a priest dedicated to honor the father of life, Ra, the sun. I do not kill."

The young man was sobbing now.

Lizla was turning in her bed, agitated by the dream, and suddenly a light woke her up.

"My lady, are you all right?" It was Iris, one of the young priestesses who attended Lizla. She had she heard Lizla cry in her sleep.

"I am all right, thank you. I had a bad dream. Maybe the eclipse is still working on my nerves." Lizla was trying to sound reassuring, while at the same time she was trying to compose herself.

Then Lizla sat in her bed and wondered about her dream. Ra-Ta being attacked? And the priests in Thebes organizing crimes against foreigners? It was similar to Mikos's story about the Hittites, she thought to herself. She was sure Mikos was just trying to scare her. He had been looking at her in a funny way, as if he wanted to approach her romantically but didn't dare, she thought. Maybe he was trying to impress her with those strange stories about foreigners.

She remembered her father Ramses IX having talked about the Hittites as being defeated by his grandfather in the famous battle of Kadesh. And following that battle, there was a treaty of peace. Maybe that was what was interwoven in her dream. Mikos's stories about foreigners attacking children and women and the other vision she had about a dark horseman who was bringing ominous news …

Something was going on, and she was being warned. She had learnt to interpret dreams as oracles. They were part of her magic classes. Ra-Ta was her teacher and mentor. He was attacked by a foreigner seeking revenge for the death of his father? What was she supposed to do about it?

Lizla could not make any sense out of it. She decided that she might try to talk to the Oracle herself. It was hard to get an appointment with her, since she was consulted by most royalty and noble classes mainly in urgent cases. But she might make some time for a royal princess. Lizla was musing on this while drinking the cup of chamomile tea that her young priestess assistant had brought her to calm her nerves. The soothing tea and the deep silence of the desert night had their effect, because she soon fell asleep.

CHAPTER 9

LIZLA MEETS HER COUSIN

Lizla arose early since she had to follow the morning exercises that preceded her Temple of Beauty class. That was part of the regime that Ishtar-la had prescribed for her before their first meeting. Lizla was a bit intimidated by Ishtar-la. She was the widow of a high Egyptian official who was half administrator and half warrior. That was a typical career path in the Egyptian ruling classes. This man, Arart, had been successful abroad and married an exotic beauty who was the second daughter of the king of Babylon.

Ishtar-la was very young when her powerful husband brought her to Memphis. In their palace, she had brought from Babylon and managed to keep a complete entourage of beauticians, masseuses, and dietitians. She wanted to make sure that her famous beauty would be for her husband to enjoy for a lifetime. But her fame had spread, and the Queen herself became enchanted with her. When Arart was killed in battle, Ishtar-la had been devastated. The Queen herself assured a restorative place for Ishtar-la in the Temple of Love at Memphis, where nobles and powerful people were aided by the famous priestesses of the Isis temple, mainly for healing and recovering from trauma.

Ishtar-la, under the auspices of the Queen herself and the high priestesses of the Isis Temple not only recovered, but felt so touched by the loving and supportive atmosphere of the Temple of Love, that she decided to dedicate her life to it. She founded the School of Beauty and was allowed to bring in her entourage. Her father in Babylon was proud of his daughter's achievement and also at the possibility of sharing some of the special gifts of the Babylonian culture with the more practical and austere Egyptians.

Lizla knew the whole story, but her own training so far was rather monastic in nature. She was destined to live in the world so she had promised Isis, and it was due to the Goddess's suggestion that Lizla had acceded to take Ishtar-la's courses in the Temple of Love. She was hoping to get married to a very special king who would understand her strange destiny, and she absolutely adored children.

But Lizla still was afraid of facing Ishtar-la. Her Babylonian friend Mizzia, although they had played together often, seemed a bit amused by Lizla's more solemn manners. Would Babylonian Ishtar-la find her manners likewise amusing?

So Lizla took the instructions given to her very seriously. Half an hour of walking in the morning, no honey cakes or sweetened figs for two weeks, and especially no beer. She did not drink that much beer, but she hated diet restrictions. Ra-Ta often had teased her on her strange combination of Ketu rising passion for freedom and her Capricorn love of discipline. But then he would add seriously, "Although many people would not understand it, that is a very good combination for leadership, and you may be a queen someday. But remember, nobody can command who does not know how to obey."

Lizla did not need much reinforcing on the subject. She was quite comfortable with discipline. It was Ishtar-la herself who intimidated her. What was she supposed to learn about love? She enjoyed Mikos's sweet, furtive looks and was annoyed by Psusennes's daring ones. She felt attracted by the Persian melodic voice, whose face she had not seen, and she felt disgusted with Altamira's slaving disposition toward her lover. Mizzia's stories of love and Annouk-Aimee's latest experiences also meant that romantic love could be dangerous. Was Ishtar-la going to teach her how to deal with men? Should she become like Aunt Lillie, the belle of all parties? Aunt Lillie was one of Ishtar-la's first disciples, but she also had a royal bearing quite Egyptian in lightness and decorum.

All these impressions were swimming in Lizla's consciousness as she did the thirty-minute walk prescribed for her. She chose the path around the man-made lake that faced the eastern oasis. When she felt sure that nobody could see her, she sat down by the lake at the end of her walk and contemplated her own face reflected in the clear lake surface. Against the pure, cloudless sky, she saw an oval face with large dark eyes and a well designed mouth, framed by the long tresses of dark hair. What was Ishtar-la going to do with this, she mused, alarmed?

Psusennes was coming from one of his hunting trips and saw his beautiful but often distant cousin looking at herself in the quiet lake's natural mirror. He decided to approach her, since he had been interrupted last time by their common mentor Ra-Ta, during his last visit to the Isis temple compound.

"Good morning, my princess. It is a beautiful day, isn't it? But not, I am sure, as priceless as the image you are seeing in the lake."

Lizla was puzzled by his gallant greeting. She felt simultaneously a bit of pride, apprehension, and delight at seeing him there, but still she reacted as if he was intruding. Psusennes was silent for a moment and kept looking at her from a respectful few feet away.

Lizla calmed down after awhile and said, smiling, "Hello, how are you? Are you on retreat?"

"No." He seemed surprised by the question. "Just visiting."

Suddenly, Lizla remembered Altamira and her impending childbirth. She did not dare to bring the subject up.

"Visit who? Ra-Ta?" she asked, to help him out of it.

"Oh, yes." The prince smiled back gratefully. "But he is in seclusion. I need to ask him for some advice," he said, and a somber shadow of irony crossed over his sun burnt face.

Lizla suddenly remembered her dream last night and wondered if she would dare to share it with her daring cousin. After all, they had the same teacher and were close relatives.

So she ventured, "Advice of a personal or political nature?" And almost distractedly, she picked up a pebble from the ground and threw it on the lake. She loved to see the flat pebble jump on the water a couple of times. When she was a child, her sisters and cousins, including Psusennes, used to compete on how many times they could make a flat pebble "jump" over a quiet pool of water. Psusennes frowned before answering. He was not used to discussing politics with women, not even one as reputedly intelligent as his royal cousin. But he had some pressing questions on his mind, and who knows, he thought, she might have some of the answers.

"Why do you ask me that? A beautiful face like yours should not get involved in such matters."

Lizla gave him a serious look. "Is Ra-Ta giving you advice on pretty faces?" She immediately bit her lip. She could not believe those unfriendly words coming from her own mouth. Psusennes smiled sheepishly.

"You got me. No. Yes, there are political issues I am worried about. It used to be so clear who your loyalties were with. Since your revered father passed away, Ramses IX, the world seems to be crumbling beneath our feet."

Psusennes looked stern and angry, but Lizla could see his sorrow beneath the bitter words.

She ventured softly, "What can Ra-Ta do about it? He is a wise man, but a priest. I never heard him talk about politics, except ..." and she stopped as she remembered her dream.

"Except what?" Now Psusennes was anxious. Almost unconsciously, he took his cousin's hand in his well-formed ones.

Lizla recoiled shyly but continued, "Well, I had a dream about him last night ..."

"Oh, just a dream." Psusennes seemed disappointed, until he remembered suddenly about Ra-Ta commenting on Lizla's psychic abilities.

"Well, yes, but it was so vivid and unusual," Lizla continued, focusing on her memories of the dream. "Of course, it may be been caused by the eclipse or perhaps also from the other political conversations I heard the last two days."

"Can you please tell me about it?" Psusennes was eager to get close to his beautiful cousin and erase the bad impressions he may have created before with his previous forwardness.

"Well, I dreamt that he was woken up by an assassin."

Psusennes tensed and raised his brows, but he said smoothly, "Please continue."

She told him how Ra-Ta had overcome the young Nubian (who was half Egyptian), taking the dagger from his hand, and how the stranger had related his need to avenge the death of his father, a Nubian official, at the hands of rebellious priests in the Thebes southern capital.

"In the dream, Ra-Ta had decided to go to Thebes to investigate the issue. What do you make of all that? Isn't it absurd, that the priests at Thebes may be conspiring against a Nubian ambassador? It does not make any sense," Lizla sighed. "But you asked to hear it." She smiled softly.

Psusennes jumped to his feel with excitement and a deeper kind of worry crossed his brow. "So that is where he went." He seemed to be thinking aloud.

Lizla asked him, "What do you mean? It was just a dream."

Her cousin jumped to his feet and forgetting all formality, he held both her hands in his. Looking into her big calm eyes, he retorted, "My dear cousin, Ra-Ta was right. You may be a prophetess. He left this morning for Thebes; they told me at the Temple. And guess what? He took a Nubian slave with him, one whose mother works at the palace." Looking deep into Lizla's astonished eyes, he stole a kiss from his surprised cousin and left.

CHAPTER 10

ISHTAR-LA—THE MISTRESS OF THE TEMPLE OF LOVE

Ishtar-la was pensive as she examined the charts of her new five disciples in the Temple of Love. Lizla was the royal princess: strange stars for a woman! Much power was indicated and psychic abilities, also healing and romance. Ishtar-la sighed. Those magnificent Egyptians! She does symbolize it all, the teacher mused to herself.

In Egypt, man and woman were seeing as equal in power. Isis defied the ruler of the universe in order to get her healing gifts. Even the ruler of life itself, Osiris himself, was brought back to life thanks to the healing power of a woman: his wife Isis.

Yes, Ishtar-la had fallen in love with Egypt many years ago. On that fateful day when she was still a young princess in the Babylonian court, this intrepid Egyptian general—a minor prince in the Memphis court—set his eyes on her for the first time. She had trembled with pleasure, pride, and a bit of fear. His gaze had been burning with admiration, respect, and a certain pride that made him irresistible. He was introduced to the Babylonian court, bringing a message of peace and alliance from Pharaoh. The king of Babylon received him as the messenger of peace from the two governments. But the moment Arart had set his eyes on Ishtar-la, his heart had been set on fire with longing and desire. It was obvious to all in the court that his feelings were making his job difficult as he submitted his considerable conciliatory messages to the king in passionate tones, all the while stealing furtive glances at Ishtar-la who—as the King's sister—was one of the queen's attendants behind the throne. The queen herself was amused with the uneasy stance of the Egyptian general turned ambassador.

"Come, Prince Arart," she said in the bewitching Babylonian style that Arart found so confusing in this royal court. In Egypt, all those about Pharaoh—particularly in an official ceremony—were guided by the high priests and yielded audience reluctantly and with the ultimate in decorum.

The queen arose, and to Ararat's surprise, she held his hand and offered him a seat next to Ishtar-la. The queen also noted with amusement that her beautiful attendant, a royal princess well traveled and experienced in the art of love and female grace, was lowering her eyes at the intense looks from the Egyptian visitor. Her burning cheeks contrasted with the rose and purple gown she wore, making her appearance more irresistible than anything Arart had ever seen before.

Nabukosodek, the king of Babylon, gave his wife a furtive glance of approval. How lucky he was to have married this beautiful queen of his. Although her beauty and subtle sensuality attracted more attention that he would prefer, he knew he could trust her.

This time, once again she had proved to be charming and politically savvy at the same time. Ishtar-la was his own younger sister. An alliance with Egypt by marrying her to the Egyptian nephew of Pharaoh would assure many months of peace, through a powerful alliance with a safe and powerful neighbor. Egypt was stable and rich; and unlike his own kingdom, the priests of Egypt respected Pharaoh, while its riches would provide a secure future for him and his family. That would help him to keep his army and palaces protected. Then, who knew? The Babylonian king gave Arart a sign of approval and acceptance as he received from the young ambassador the beautiful painted box full of jewels that he had brought from Egypt. Then he took a ring out of his own hand and put it in the small finger of Arart, who then bowed to the Babylonian king, kissing his hand.

Ishtar-la was lost in her reveries as she contemplated their beautiful memories together. During the next two weeks, Arart had courted her intensely and at the third week, a marriage of both political alliance and of young love made her feel she was living in paradise.

A month later, the happy newlyweds returned to Egypt carrying a pact of alliance for the Pharaoh and a new beautiful exotic princess to grace the Egyptian courts, Arart's palace, and his own heart.

Ishtar-la always remembered those sunny days with love and gratitude. Although five years later, her husband was killed in battle defending Pharaoh's forces against the Assyrians, she had found a new home in Memphis. While she had received a Babylonian education, her mother was Egyptian by birth, and Ishtar-la always dreamt with visiting her mother's place of birth. Also the understanding of the Egyptians' more serene manners, constant purification rituals, and other aspects of their strange religion was her secret initiation from her mother. Besides, she felt also inclined to guide the young Egyptian princesses in the arts of makeup and to appreciate the opportunity to learn new hair styles and more colorful clothing, which the young girls found fascinating. The priestesses of the Temple of Isis were looking to restore the old custom of the Temple of Love, to supplement the Temple of Healing. The Temple of Love was more like psychic and emotional frustrations healing center, as well as a place of preparation for marriage and motherhood.

When Ishtar-la became a young widow of twenty-three, a high priestess of the Temple of Isis asked her to take over direction of the Temple of Love.

This had happened ten years ago. Since then, many young princesses, priests' family members, rich and powerful businessmen, and other members of the powerful classes, tried to get their daughters into this prestigious school of love at the Memphis Isis Temple. Only a few where admitted every year, and within that privileged group already a more select group was to work directly with Ishtar-la as her own private disciples.

Ishtar-la dropped her memories now as she looked in the mirror made of polished bronze. Now thirty-three, she retained a striking beauty that combined the best of her Babylonian upbringing and her mother's and husband's Egyptian refinement.

Her Babylonian training had helped her, in her own quiet and personal way, to convey the ability to open up the hearts of her different disciples who came from many different cultures and backgrounds. She was happy and successful in her work. But a woman's heart is a woman's heart, she said to herself, while she devoutly glanced at her favorite statue of the Goddess Ishtar, and sneaked a brief glance at the magnificent picture of Isis hanging on the wall of the Temple corridor.

Sometimes she felt some special groups were challenging. Today's group filled her with apprehension. Lizla was in line for royal ascension. Rumor had it that Psusennes, a second cousin of Lizla's through being born to the late Pharaoh's younger sister, was in love with her. Psusennes was also a favorite disciple of Ra-Ta, the highest priest in Memphis, who acknowledged having given Lizla initiation into the Egyptian mysteries. What powers did Lizla have, and what would be her promised, exalted future? Ra—Ta would never talk to Ishtar-la; he was inaccessible to women, the palace rumors said, but he had been kind enough to send her a copy of Lizla's astrological chart. Did that really mean he agreed with the training? Ishtar-la wondered to herself, rather amused. The old Babylonian ways and humor took over as she regarded it funny to find any man who was afraid of women, no matter how holy such a man might be. He'd better be a priest, she laughed inwardly.

Now Ishtar-la reviewed the chart of her other new disciples: Lakshmi was Suryananda's daughter, a bright girl brought up in the tradition of an Indian Brahmin family. Curiously, she had an open mind and a flair for business. Maybe that was why she was transplanted to a rich country like Egypt. An interesting challenge to develop thought Ishtar-la, since Brahmins were very zealous of their caste system and their sacred mission as custodians of their millenarian wisdom. But the Priests of Thebes had similar concerns. Ishtar-la made a note to include several trips to Thebes within their learning programs.

Annouk-Aimee was Mikos's and Diogenes's younger sister. She had recently been seduced by an Assyrian and she was pregnant, so some healing and preparation for motherhood surely was indicated in her training. The other two girls were Gemeti and Suma, twin sisters born of the Babylonian aristocracy. They were the daughters of the Babylonian ambassador. Ishtar-la had a close relationship with the embassy and the ambassador's family. She knew they were particularly eager to see their daughters being educated in the Temple of Love by such a successful priestess and teacher, a fellow Babylonian teacher who would provide a bridge of culture and emotional understanding for the foreign upbringing of their daughters.

It was not easy living in Egypt as a foreigner, particularly for the privileged classes. Egyptians were famously proud of their civilization's success and had as well a strong sense of decorum or "ma'at" which covered every aspect of their lives. Bathing twice a day, wearing very thin linen garments of white or purple code colors, depending on the occasion and level of prestige and power of the individual their lifestyle was very formal and somewhat threatening or boring to a foreigner. Babylonians were used to warmer clothes of multiple colors, elaborate ornaments and heavier food, which made them often overweight and somewhat uncivilized by the Egyptian standards of desert lightness.

Living in the desert climate creates fears of the heat and leads to much-needed protection against the dryness and even mortal power of the desert sun. That was part of the reason behind the lightness of the clothing and diet and the frequent bathing. The unique Egyptian form of government was a unified theocracy supported by an elaborate caste of powerful priests and princesses. This created and confirmed the rather rigid but very stable family and political traditions of the Egyptian culture. Most of the foreigners from all around Egypt who came to visit, study, or stay commented on their difficulty in adapting their Greek, Nubian, Indian, or Babylonian mores. They came from more nomadic races, or they were farmers from multiple season lands. They found it difficult to integrate into this Egyptians pyramid-like monolithic culture where they felt politely tolerated but often not welcome.

Ishtar-la was very aware of this problem, as she had experienced it firsthand. However, she had had her own Egyptian background and the love and protection of her rich and powerful Egyptian husband. She suspected that was which had made the transition not as difficult for her as it would be for the new disciples. Ishtar—la remembered her mother's admonition, which coincided with her own mentor, the high priestess of the Temple of Isis's: "When in doubt about issues of the heart, especially when women are concerned, turn to Isis."

CHAPTER 11

THE MYSTERIES OF EGYPTIAN LOVE

Ishtar-la looked apologetically to her small statue of the Goddess Ishtar, the Babylonian Goddess of womanhood, and prayed: "I will turn to Isis as I believe here in Egypt both you and her are the one." Then with her rich melodious voice, she intoned the Isis invocation.

Soon she went quietly into meditation. A rosy glow in her heart let her know that her question was being answered.

"Mother of Love," said a sweet voice full of musical tones, with both authority and compassion, "Whom do you seek?" Ishtar-la was startled; she expected some form of inspiration, but not a direct answer. A swift thought of concern ran through her mind. She remembered earlier teachers in her own country guarding against demons and possession. But this voice was healing and reassuring, seeming to spring from her own heart.

"Who are you?" Ishtar-la asked in a trembling voice, filled with awe and astonishment.

"Mother of Love, do not fear. Your loving concern for these five girls entrusted to your care in my Temple of Love and Healing is very pleasing to me. I am Isis, whom you invoked. Are you looking for guidance?"

Ishtar-la took a deep breath and replied reverently: "Well, yes, I find this task challenging. They are all so different, and it seems that there is so much at stake."

The Goddess smiled. Ishtar-la could not see her smile, but somehow she felt she caught it in the Goddess's voice.

"Yes, indeed, you are right on both counts," the Goddess continued, "but you have your own ability as a devout and loving woman to guide them in what they need to learn from you, and in that, they are not very different. Do you see?"

Ishtar-la felt she heard right and that she had understood, but decided to ask for further guidance.

"And what is it that they have in common, that I can find in them, pray please tell me?"

The Goddess answered in a more authoritative and solemn tone now: "Well, it is in the mystery of womanhood and the power of this mystery, where I will guide you. Please go to the Temple library and get a book that I will leave there for you. Ask the librarian. You have my blessings now."

And the soft rose glow disappeared, leaving behind an exquisite perfume like jasmine. Exhausted, Ishtar-la fell asleep.

Two hours later, she woke up and went up to the library. She was astonished again, as the librarian was ready with her present.

"Who gave this to you?" inquired Ishtar-la; still not sure the whole thing was not a dream.

"A young boy with a Persian accent who said this was a present for you from a foreign queen." Then the librarian was interrupted in her explanation as she turned around to answer a student's insistent question. The young girl librarian was a bit afraid she had offended the princess.

Ishtar-la smiled and said, "Don't worry; it is fine. Let me have the package." As she unwrapped her present, the most beautiful picture of Isis and Osiris holding hands was engraved on the cover of the papyrus box that contained the roll. Under the picture was a note written in golden sacred hieroglyphics: “The Mysteries of Egyptian Love”. Ishtar-la took the sacred gift and returned to her palace.

Chapter 12

Ishtar-la's Gift

Unbeknownst to each other, Lizla and Annouk-Aimee had the same idea: to take a stroll around the forest that surrounded the man-made lake on the western side of the temple. Lizla loved trees. They were a rarity in the Egyptian climate, and only the richest and most powerful people could have a profusion of them to gather shade for men, flowers, and lovers. The Temple of Love had several groves of trees. Some of them produced fruits like orange and pomegranate, while others gave figs and olives. But Lizla's favorite grove was the one with the magnolia trees, an exotic specimen imported from China. Their fragrance was magnificent, and somehow she had felt drawn to them as she remembered the first time she had seen Altamira and her cousin in a passionate embrace under those trees. Lizla felt her cheeks burning at the memory and quickly sat down on a fallen tree trunk to open the papyrus preparation material she had received from Ishtar-la as an introduction to the first Temple of Love lesson.

She was happy to see the Isis invocation at the very beginning of the scroll. That calmed some of her original apprehension. Having a Babylonian teacher, even one as refined as Ishtar-la, was a concern for a royal Egyptian princess. But this familiar invocation seemed both an invitation to trust as well as a blessing from the Goddess.

All of a sudden, she heard steps coming from behind her. Rolling back her papyrus, Lizla sat up in rapt attention. Singing a soft Greek love song, Annouk-Aimee was strolling with delight as she entered the famous magnolia tree grove, favorite of lovers and poets. She was absentmindedly collecting the pretty fragrant flowers and adding them to the tresses of her golden hair. Then she sat down by the pool and looked at her bright blue eyes and blonde tresses that revealed a fair skin and a serious disposition. She also noticed the dark circles under her eyes that she was not used to seeing in her former self, when she was in her beloved Greek home, and a spectrum of fear ran through her. How she missed her mother and the more free-flowing manners of her native country! People were given to sports of mind and body, for every Greek that had the good fortune of attending a good Greek school like she and her brothers had, had developed a healthy love of debate and competition: both on the horse racing trail, as well as with the many sports of the javelin, archery, and fencing. Even the ladies participated in argumentative debates, at least the most adventurous and intelligent ladies.

But here in Egypt, everything was regulated. Even the chariots and horses were adorned by the nobles in elaborate ceremonies. Everything was a ritual, and it created order and security, but sometimes, she would have preferred the more spontaneous rhythms of her old country.

She was surprised to find Lizla sitting on the trunk of a fallen tree, holding a copy of the same papyrus roll with the golden cord ending in purple silk buttons that she had received from Ishtar-la that very morning. Lizla saluted her politely, but was somehow distant. She liked her, but she was Mikos's younger sister, and Lizla did not know how much Mikos had shared with his sister about their strange encounter in the underground pyramid of light. Lizla was young enough to fear being different. Somehow, her spiritual and mystical experiences made her fear isolation from other people, particularly when they were obviously scheduled to be classmates. But she did not need to fear. Mikos's rational nature was even more apprehensive than Lizla's about sharing his own hardly-understood psychic experiences with his own family. Lizla suspected as much when she encountered the clear blue eyes of her new classmate, greeting her with a humble, "Good morning, Princess Lizla." There was nothing in that look to suspect that her secret had been betrayed.

Lizla embraced her friend Mikos's sister with what seemed to the Greek girl surprising candor. Princess Lillie had always maintained a respectful but rather haughty distance with her in spite of being her older brother's lover.

But Lizla asked eagerly, "Hello, my friend, how are you doing? You must be feeling rather homesick, here in our strange land? How is Mikos? I have not seen him in the last few days."

Annouk-Aimee returned the embrace and smile with a warm and thankful heart. "I have not seen him either. I think he is quite enthralled with his studies of Yoga and Astrology. He was talking of following Suryananda when he returns to India next year," she answered shyly, not knowing if she had revealed too much of his brother's plans.

But Lizla laughed heartily! "Ah, Mikos your brother soaks knowledge like a sponge, and I am sure he will feel more comfortable in India with their intense theories and elaborate diagrams." Suddenly, Annouk-Aimee felt an intense liking for Lizla. How sweet and beautiful she was, and how accurately she had described her brother's studious nature.

"It seems like we are in the same class," Lizla continued as she saw Annouk-Aimee holding the golden laced papyrus with the Temple of Love seal engraved on the outer border.

"Yes, and it seems we both have the same teachings to study it under these perfumed trees," Annouk-Aimee ventured, admiring the gorgeous surroundings.

Lizla answered, "I don't understand much of it, but I hope it will be explained in class. I know the Isis invocation, at least, so I am confident that the teachings are going to be consistent with our previous ones."

Annouk-Aimee smiled shyly. "Your previous ones?" she thought to herself, not daring to reveal her secret apprehension. The mystic invocations were a source of uneasiness as well as wonder. Lizla saw the frown on her new friend and put her hand on Annouk-Aimee's shoulder.

"I have a favor to ask you," Lizla said reassuringly. "Would you please teach me Greek? I am sure my father would pay you."

Annouk-Aimee smiled gratefully. "It would be an honor for me, Royal Princess," she answered." Lizla was also curious about her new friend's pregnancy, but she did not dare to ask. Finally she ventured, "How are you feeling?"

Annouk-Aimee blushed, but she did not avoid the issue. "I am assuming Mikos told you … Well, it was stupid of me, I guess, but he also probably told you that I was always a bit reckless … younger sister of three older brothers."

Lizla thought she had seen it often in the palace. Same thing with Altamira, she could not help a frown as she remembered her cousin's lover … But she changed her frown to a reassuring smile when she saw Annouk-Aimee's discomfort. She tried to put an arm around her, but it was too late. The Greek girl said she had to leave promptly and respectfully said farewell.

Lizla was puzzled. She would have to be more careful with this girl. She did not mean to hurt her feelings."She is surely bashful for a reckless character," Lizla thought.

Quietly, she returned to her strange preliminary homework.

After the Isis invocation, the papyrus had a picture of a human body, which was outlined as a female form. Soon she realized that the inner drawings' explanations corresponded to the information she had learned about in her spiritual training. She was curious about it.

Ra-Ta's training had been verbal, and he had never shown her any pictures or diagrams. He insisted that inner knowledge should be acquired through meditation alone. So what were those pictures? Lizla was puzzled; it seemed there was more to those chakras than the circles or wheels in the *Ka*. Could one find them in a human body? She would have to ask Ishtar-la about that.

She had taken basic anatomy courses before and remembered earlier sneaking into one of her Uncle Ptolemy's private libraries, the uncle that was obsessed with death and embalming. That was the only time she had seen text with pictures about the body like this. She wished she was back at the palace in Tanis, so she could sneak back into her uncle's libraries again. Lizla's curiosity was insatiable. But then she thought that the Isis Temple must have a library, since it had two schools: the Temple of Healing and the Temple of Love. At any rate, it was interesting in the pictures that the chakras were connected to the physical organs in the body. Would this course contain classes in medicine? Lizla was also very curious about that. She had training in spiritual healing, but her knowledge of medicine was rudimentary and mainly about the muscles and skin rashes.

Lizla suddenly felt hungry. She went back to the Temple grounds and returned to her room to bathe and change for dinner.

Ishtar-la was fascinated with her new discovery, received at the library: The ivory box cover that had the golden engraving of an Ankh, the Cross of Life, contained three papyruses. The first one said Structures of the *Ka*; the second one and the third one were encased in a silver cylinder container and were merely marked: To be opened only when the first scroll is completed.

Ishtar-la was a little annoyed at this. "How do they know when I finished?" she said to herself, and she tried to open the two tubes in vain. She thought of asking someone to help her, but she could not find an explanation of how the precious box had come to her. Magic was not familiar territory for Ishtar-la. She was a wise and devout woman, but she preferred to leave the supernatural realms to priests and diviners. Her earlier training was also riddled with a superstitious fear of the unknown like the presence of demons and evil entities …

Carefully, she un-wrapped the first scroll and saw it contained several sections. The first one was marked: "Instructions to the Teacher" and was written in three languages—the sacred Egyptian hieroglyphic, Persian, and Greek. She was familiar with Persian as part of her princess training in Babylon, and of course, she was well versed in Egyptian hieroglyphics from her mother's heritage and recent Temple work. The manuscript had a picture of a female form with description and explanations of the chakras. In a different section she found a picture of an astrological chart, which she remembered coincided with hers. Again her superstitious fear made her put the scroll aside. How did that happen? Who has the magic? Who had her chart? Her name was not mentioned at all. It simply said, "Teacher's Sample Chart". Then there was another diagram where the two pictures were combined, with specific instructions on breathing exercises. The legend underneath that picture said "The Flow of Love Power".

Then there was another section with physical exercises and a demonstration of Hatha Yoga and Persian calisthenics that was supposed to be the prelude for the training session.

Ishtar-la was very mystified by this gift. She knew it was part of her task to impart this knowledge to her young audience. But why obtain a special gift from the Goddess like this? It was incredibly auspicious. That book seemed beyond the general "Princesses training "she was used to give. What did it mean? May be some of her disciples will become an expert in Kundalini in the future or she will discover the ancient mysteries of the *Ka*?

Ishtar-la wrapped the book with care and put it in the golden treasure box that contained her most precious memories from home and husband. Maybe someday, she felt sure; the book would become an instrument of discovery for herself and for the school mission.

Chapter 13

The Temple of Love

The Temple of Love was located in the middle of the three tree groves that flanked the eastern horizon of the Isis Temple compound. It had a magnificent entrance where five major columns surrounded the Isis sculpture. This statue of the Goddess was twenty-five feet in height, and her luminous eyes had been designed in shining dark lapis lazuli. Much commentary surrounded that decision, but it was ironically Ra-Ta's influence that had prevailed to give the Goddess of Love dark blue eyes, just like the olden legends said the ancient sages had envisioned the Goddess. Her body was made of translucent rose alabaster.

The Temple of Love was a new construction and so was the statue. Lizla reflected on this coincidence, as it was the first day of the year, just two months before her fifteenth birthday. It gave her a sense of relief. A lot of the girls at her age were already married. Her gorgeous younger sister had a child already, but Lizla would be fifteen and still in school. The calendar for the Temple of Love graduation program was three years, and she would be a grown up woman by then and could choose her own husband, or so she hoped. What she did not know was that Ra-Ta, her mother, and the Pharaoh had already arranged that. The political situation was unstable, her stars marked a strange destiny, and Lizla would be better off marrying at a mature age when her studies had been completed and she would be sure of her own needs and direction. Once married, a Pharaonic coronation would be imminent. The prince consort should be the ideal Pharaoh to share her throne.

The trumpets heralded the birth of Ra over the horizon, and the morning procession began. The high priestess of the Isis Temple went before her train of younger priestesses, leading them through a corridor of burning candles that trailed the passage from the main temple to the Temple of Love. The trail of beautiful priestesses behind her were resplendent under the sun, as they were adorned in their best clothes and each one carried a tray of flowers, a burning candle made of pure beeswax, and a small gold container of saffron rice and barley signifying beauty, light, and abundance. The high priestess's arms were bare, and her white linen tunic was enhanced with a silk shawl of luminous purple, simply adorned with a heavy necklace of gold and lapis lazuli. Like her attendants, her hair was adorned with a jasmine garland that fell behind her down to her waist. When the high priestesses arrived at the new statue to inaugurate the Temple of Love school year, she stopped, raised her eyes, and intoned the Isis Invocation. When she finished, she stood silently and signaled her attendants. They surrounded her in a semi-circle and started chanting a love hymn to God, Love, and the sustaining power of the universe. All the while, they were waving the trails in unison. The priests of the Ra Temple, the students and their families, some royal princes, including Princess Lillie and the queen, Lizla's mother, were attending the ceremony from the Temple balcony. They were all touched by the beauty and devotion of the priestesses and stood in reverent silence. When the priestesses finished their chants, they bowed to the magnificent statue and deposited the offering trays with their burning lights by the small wall that surrounded the statue. A small pond had been created around the statue, which those walls contained. From their veranda on the Temple's second floor, Lizla could see her mother trying to hide her tears. The queen did not notice her reflection in the small pond, but Lizla's heart understood. She would have to return to the royal palace in Tanis and work on the political schemes that would support the legitimate royal lineage against the Thebes priests' ambitious and the Nubian ways. Lizla felt grateful for Mother and silently asked Isis to protect her family.

When the ceremony was completed, the students returned to their classes. In the distance she noticed Mikos entering the Temple of Healing, which was the School of Medicine. Ra-Ta went back to the Amon-Ra Temple, and Lizla surrounded Ishtar-la with her new classmates.

The sun rays were powerful even in the early morning, and in spite of the protective shade of the trees, students, teachers, and visitors were grateful to obtain refuge from the desert heat. The Temple of Love's new construction was indeed beautiful. Ishtar-la's private classroom where they would hold classes with her private disciples was up on a small hill covered with trees and flowers. A small pond was behind a grove of palm trees, and benches had been built around it. Classes could be given indoors or outdoors, as the weather and the curriculum dictated. Ishtar-la led her special group of direct disciples through a long corridor that ended up in the large auditorium. Inside the auditorium there were assembled all the students of the different classes: Anatomy, Art, Music, Weaving, Nursery, and Cooking.

Ishtar-la addressed the whole assembly and welcomed them to the new Temple of Love. She was surprised at the diversity of the group. She had not personally welcome half of them, but as the pressure of priests, nobles, and other powerful people kept on mounting, she had allowed for new concessions to expand the curriculum and the audience.

The Temple of Isis was famous for beauty classes, and many a young noble girl from Upper and Lower Egypt, Palestine, Greece, Crete, Caledonia, the Nubian, and the Hittite lands were attracted to the school. Ishtar-la was both anxious and grateful at the same time.

Maybe this was indeed larger than she expected. Her fame had spread before they even started the new Temple of Love program.

Her classes had been private in her own palace before then. What if she failed?

"It is not up to you alone," her inner voice reassured her. "Bless them all and let them start."

So she did; she introduced the teachers, showed a map of the compound, discussed the rules of discipline, and the timetable for the whole school and disbanded the assembly to go to their respective classes.

Lizla and Lakshmi stood quietly behind her. Ishtar-la turned around and smiled at her special disciples and embraced each one of them. Alas, that gesture of tenderness would be the last for many days to come, she realized. Her position as teacher and school headmistress precluded any special gestures to any disciple.

Immediately, talking in a stately voice, she announced to the disciples, "Let us begin."

The group stood up silently and followed Ishtar-la to their appointed classroom. Ishtar-la led her group through a candlelit corridor that was sumptuously painted with pictures of Isis, Osiris, Ishtar, Horus, and other gods and goddesses of their different spiritual traditions. Lizla was surprised about that and a little alarmed. What was she getting into? Wasn't this the Isis Temple? This exalted lady had a special reputation in Pharaohs' court, but she was still a foreigner.

Ishtar-la arrived at her classroom and ordered her attendants to arrange the cushions on chairs in a semi-circle. The teacher's desk was on a higher stand and a large board covered with fine linens had some pictures that filtered dimly through. The sunlight was diffused in marvelous pink and soft blue colors through the stained glass windows.

Ishtar-la asked her disciples to sit down and with a warm smile said, "First of all, let us get to know each other. Please one by one, introduce yourselves, your family situation, country of origin, religion, and main reason for seeking the wisdom of the Temple of Love training."

The disciples were a bit taken aback.

Ishtar-la said, "Any volunteers to go first?"

Lizla's natural leadership overcame her resistance. She raised her hand, saying: "I will start. Please, here in the classroom, can we please dispense with our titles, just using first names?"

Ishtar-la nodded in agreement.

Lizla continued: "My name is Lizla; I am the daughter of Ramses IX who was killed in battle then years ago." Ishtar-la took a deep breath, as that was the battle where her own beloved husband had been killed trying to protect Pharaoh, but she held her peace. "I am of marrying age, but also in line for the throne of Egypt," Lizla continued. "Most of the decisions on my education and travel are arranged by my parents and teachers. I am eager to learn and would follow any training that does not interfere with my duty or religion." Lizla's strong stance brought a suppressed cry of disbelief from Gemeti and Suma, a quiet smile from Annouk-Aimee, and a look of quiet admiration from Lakshmi.

Ishtar-la answered with a quiet nod. "Next to the right, please" she said.

Gemeti answered, "My name is Gemeti; I was born in Babylon of a family descended from royal lineage. My father is the Ambassador of Babylon in Egypt. My parents decide on my education, my destiny, and my marriage. I am currently betrothed to a diplomat, so I am assuming royal court duties, and female wisdom is in my future," she added with a smile.

Suma continued, "I am Gemeti's twin sister; I am also betrothed to a high official in court."

Annouk-Aimee was next. "My name is Annouk-Aimee; I came here to Egypt to further my education and to provide family support for my brothers, Diogenes and Mikos. I was born in Greece."

Finally, Lakshmi introduced herself: "My name is Lakshmi, which is the name of the Indian Goddess of Fortune. My parents decided to educate me in Egypt to learn the ways of wealth and to support my parents and my future husband in their sacred duties. I am a Brahmini (a female Brahmin)."

Ishtar-la noticed with quiet and sympathetic amusement the different forms of pride that each one of these initial introductions was revealing. She added, "Thank you very much. As for me, my name is Ishtar-la, and I was born in Babylon. My father was the late Babylonian king so I was naturally selected to become one of the queen's favorite attendants. I met my husband in Babylon. He was a minor prince of Egypt who came to offer a pact of alliance to my king and brother, from the Pharaoh. But we both fell in love, and I was allowed to marry him and followed him to Memphis." Ishtar-la's devotion to her late husband and his and her new country were obvious in the strange shine in her eyes. Tears were showing and the hearts of her new disciples melted with romantic inspirations.

Ishtar-la recovered herself quickly and facing all of them, she stood up. "Now my dear ladies, what is your first impression of this class? What do you think would be our greatest goal and also our greatest challenge?"

Lizla saw the opportunity to voice her concern, so she immediately raised her hand: "Well, for one, we are all from different backgrounds, traditions, and religions." She took a deep breath and continued: "Isn't education, including love, taught differently for each one of us?" Lizla's eyes were not defiant, but her zeal was obvious in her speech. Ishtar-la was glad to see her demonstrate her leadership in such a courageous and polished way.

"She will make a great Egyptian queen some day," Ishtar-la thought to herself, "and I will be proud of her, I am sure." Then she looked at the other girls who were uncomfortably squirming in their seats in nervous expectation.

Lakshmi volunteered, "Well, in my country we have over five hundred languages and many religions, but the basic truths tend to be common. That is why we preach tolerance." She said this firmly but not too aggressively.

Ishtar-la liked her second disciple too. This was going to be an interesting class.

Annouk-Aimee ventured, "Well, ever since I came here, I have been exposed to the strange methods and beliefs of the Egyptian people. It makes me feel homesick sometimes and a bit constrained. In my country everything is questioned and debated … but we also value learning. I have learned a lot so far, and I look forward to be improved by your wisdom." She felt sympathy for Ishtar-la's position as a teacher of such a privileged group of strong ladies.

Ishtar-la took a deep breath and said quietly, "Thank you for being so frank. You are indeed right in your perceptions but also need some expansion. That is what true learning is all about. Regarding religion and education, no one can take that away from you. All forms of loyalty to your true gods will bring you closer to heaven, and that is independent of belief type. The true values of faith, commitment, discipline, valor, humility, patience and all the virtues that make a woman priceless are exalted in all traditions. But the most important things, you will find out are not our differences, but our similarities. You will take several classes in medicine, beauty, astronomy, astrology, flower arrangement, weaving, and other related feminine arts. You may not need them all, but in your positions as rulers or wives of rulers and officers of the court, you need the information about how to manage and evaluate services and situations. Above all, being a woman is the foundation of the family structure. Our future kings learn to fight and hunt in their fathers' chariots. They learn how to understand hearts and souls in their mothers' eyes."

CHAPTER 14

ANATOMY OF THE KA LESSON

Ishtar-la asked the students to open the papyrus books they had received before the class started. Each one of the paper boxes was adorned with a cross of life and the Temple of Love seal. The box was marked "Class I Anatomy of the *Ka* and the Flow of the Prana."

Taking the cover of the Teacher's Copy, which had the same engraving in golden hieroglyphics, Ishtar-la asked her pupils. "Do you know what this title means?" Both Lizla and Lakshmi raised their hands, almost in unison. Ishtar-la turned to Lizla first and said, "Well?"

Lizla said confidently: "The *Ka* is our own inner personal soul; the prana is its energy. I am assuming we are going to learn how this flow works. I have experienced it in meditation, but have no idea of what happens, just the feeling of it."

Lizla stopped and looked around timidly. She had the tendency to do that. She would get all fired up on some new idea, and then realize she had found the wrong audience. "Bad for a future Queen," she said inwardly to herself. So she kept quiet, looking at the floor.

But her teacher did not share Lizla's concern. She was happy to have advanced disciples, so she said, "Excellent. This is a great introduction, because, yes, we will learn both the theory and the practical application of the teachings. And thank you for being forward with your personal experience." Then addressing the group class, she added: "All of you have been selected for your future key positions of leadership. This is powerful, sacred knowledge that is not given lightly, and very rarely to women. So please, be aware that you can speak freely. You all have sworn a vow of secrecy about these sacred teachings. That makes this class a safe place to learn and to share." Turning to Lakshmi, the teacher gave her a signal to speak.

"Well, my father is my teacher and Guru. Some of his teachings are secret too, but the experience that Lizla describes is also part of our philosophy in India. I have learnt to meditate and understand Prana as the vital force that animates the psychic body. Is that what you call the *Ka* in Egypt?"

Ishtar-la's eyes were very shiny with approval as she nodded affirmatively, with a quiet smile.

Lakshmi continued, "The Prana circulates the Shakti that is the vital energy through a series of channels called Nadis."

Ishtar-la made a sign of approval, but then raised her hand for Lakshmi to stop. "Excellent too, but we are getting ahead of ourselves." She then turned to the other disciples. Annouk-Aimee, Gemeti and Suma, were wide open and a bit taken aback at the superior knowledge of their classmates.

Ishtar-la said to re-assure them, "This will be explained in class, and exercises will help you to understand it all. Don't worry for now."

Annouk-Aimee said, "My brother had an Indian teacher who taught him Yoga. He used to talk to me about Prana. When I was younger I was quite restless and often got into trouble."

The girls giggled. Annouk-Aimee felt the rush of blood to her cheeks, but she continued, "Mikos, my brother, would tell me to take deep breaths to balance my Prana."

"Excellent point," said Ishtar-la. "That is a good place to start. Please seat yourselves comfortably, and close your eyes. Now take a deep breath and exhale."

The girls followed her instructions.

"Now inhale again, very slowly and deeply, and then wait a second. Now exhale long and pause for another second. Do this three times more."

The room was quiet with the centered breathing. The birds chirping on the orange blossoms were the only sound coming from outside, and the blue rose light that the stained glass windows filtered from the morning sun filled the teacher with an incredible feeling of fulfillment. She had only a first class with this new group, but something told her a whole year of wonder was awaiting them all.

After a while, Ishtar-la told her disciples, "Don't open your eyes yet. Please look into your bodies. Can you feel any difference?" A second later she said, "Open your eyes, and please share."

Gemeti raised her hand timidly. "I did not see anything in my body. I felt more peaceful, but I can only look outside with my eyes open." Suma, her twin sister, could not help a giggle.

Annouk-Aimee laughed more heartily and agreed. "I had the same problem, but I felt something; my inner chest seemed to expand and I felt peaceful and, please do not laugh, but I had a clear sensation that I felt my stomach empty."

Suma laughed loudly now. "You mean you felt hungry?

"No, I mean I have been having an upset stomach the last few weeks, but now it seemed to have settled down somehow." Annouk-Aimee was truly uneasy now. She did not want to reveal the details of her pregnancy, which she hoped was a secret to everyone else but the teacher.

Ishtar-la took over the conversation gently. "Very good. The sensation of peace that Gemeti described is expected. How many of you felt quieter?" All hands went up.

Lakshmi ventured, "I think my heart stopped for a minute."

Ishtar-la smiled again. "Perfect. That is all we were doing with this exercise. Like Lakshmi pointed out earlier, the Prana is depending on the breath that at the same time does circulate the energy through the *Ka*. It also has control over the mind, because it feeds the energy of the mind. The mind has an influence over the human heart, so when the Prana is controlled, like we did a few moments ago, the mind slows down and sends calming messages to the body. That in turn tends to produce a healing effect on the body, like the release of Annouk-Aimee's stomach tension and a feeling of peace. Any questions?"

Annouk-Aimee raised her hand. She had always needed a rational explanation. "I can understand the feeling of it, but I don't understand why?" she asked.

The disciples looked at her incredulously. What did she mean by why? That is the way the *Ka* worked, the teacher had said, and that is the way it felt in their experience. Lakshmi and Lizla gave each other the look of secret bemusement that often students feel when they are more advanced than their peers. Gemeti and Suma were reluctant to look up. The gods knew how humans worked, they thought, so it was not wise to ask why. They believed that perhaps you should be grateful for this knowledge. But Ishtar-la had been exposed to Mediterranean teachers and books before and had always admired their inquisitive minds.

She answered the intrepid blue-eyed girl who was so daring in her questioning: "Good question, Annouk-Aimee. There is a reason for every scientific fact like the working of our minds, souls, and bodies. That is why schools exist—to make people understand these natural laws and learn to live more in harmony with God's creation. Understanding and knowledge are pleasing to heaven, and the gods of wisdom bless our minds when we are eager to learn."

Annouk-Aimee could not help a look of victory over her more subdued classmates. Lakshmi remembered her own father saying that too. This made her feel much at home from then on, even with this strange Egyptian classroom with a Babylonian teacher and foreign classmates. "A Brahmin is the guardian of sacred knowledge" was the motto her family always taught her. "Strange are the ways of the gods, to fulfill destiny" Lakshmi remembered that her father often said that too.

Addressing Annouk-Aimee, Ishtar-la said, "It always is good to ask questions because the subject is complex, and it may take you many classes to understand it fully. Different disciplines and much life experience are required to get all the answers you would like. In this case, it is an excellent question. The mind is one of the four psychic instruments that make a human *Ka* truly human. The mind creates thoughts which generate words. We use those words outwardly when spoken or written to communicate with others. Inwardly the words of our mind give commands to the body. They are mostly unconscious to us, but not to the body. It is hard to control the mind, but it can be accessed through control of the Prana." Then she added, looking at the sand-clock, "We are running out of time, so I am giving you an exercise for homework. Over the next three days, find and spend ten minutes each day doing this exercise. Select a steady sitting posture, do the breathing exercise we practiced today with your eyes closed, and then examine your thoughts. Write them down in the papyrus book pages that are blank, in the second half of the book. This will be your class workbook. May the gods bless you in your studies. Class dismissed."

Five days later, Ishtar-la received her disciples for the second lesson. She asked them, "How did the exercise go?"

Gemeti and Suma recoiled. They had been very busy attending their parents' celebration of their brother's wedding. Many people came from Babylon, their native city, and the two ladies had been playing hostess almost without stopping. Gemeti recalled that even the magnificent embassy gardens where she used to take refuge with her friends and lately with her fiancée, were invaded by children playing games. There also constant streams of astonished visitors who could not stop wondering how such a marvel of trees, flowers, and fountain beds could grow in the middle of the desert. For that reason, twice right before dinner, Gemeti had stopped and retired to her chambers to contemplate the lesson and apply it to center herself, as she felt drained by the intense political and busy atmosphere that surrounded the ambassador's residence.

Gemeti had found out that her breathing exercises brought peace and calm for a while, but eventually a dull ache in her heart reminded her of her beloved's absence. He had gone to Babylon to organize the trip of his family to Egypt. The family was coming to the wedding because the son of the Babylonian ambassador was marrying a cousin of Pharaoh. Such an occasion would be an ideal time to introduce his own fiancée to his mother and father. Gemeti had agreed to her mother's plan and was both excited and a bit nervous to meet her future in-laws.

"Thank you. That is a very good example," Ishtar-la congratulated Gemeti after she shared her homework experience with the group. Ishtar-la continued, "Breathing control is one essential of the practical side of book knowledge which you receive in school. Not only does it help you to relax, but it also protects you from the tensions of the multiple challenges our lives bring continuously. All of us in this room have court or official functions. Our lives are not private, and everything we do, say, eat, or wear is scrutinized. This is particularly true in Egypt where 'ma'at' or decorum is the basic—often applied unspoken—rule. This sense of harmony must be present in all aspects of public life—at least the appearance of it. So your training in breath control can pay for itself in everyday stress reduction." She stopped and waited for her disciples' comments.

Lizla was not satisfied. Stress control was fine, but she needed to know more. That was why she was going to school. She had experience with the inner chakras and had heard enough about the Prana, which was supposed to contain marvelous wisdom. Much wonderful knowledge was hidden, so she had heard, in those mysterious inner works of the body and the soul.

She ventured, "I tried the exercises, but as I am used to meditating, after a few rounds, I went into a trance. Then it was hard to keep it to ten minutes, since I had an urge to continue to meditate."

Ishtar-la looked serious as she replied, "So what did you do?"

"I opened my eyes and reflected on the experiences, recording them in my journal," Lizla sighed.

"Good," said Ishtar-la rather severely, "for this is not a religion class. However, you need to understand well the workings of the body, so your spiritual experiences bring only clarity to your mind and heart. There is nothing holy about confusion." Ishtar-la, finished the last sentence with a consoling smile, but still Lizla felt rebuked. She did understand, however, her new teacher's concerns. The meaning of the exercise was becoming clearer to her now.

The other disciples related different experiences of memory recollections and or relaxation.

Suma said a bit defiantly, "I am new to all this. I tried these once or twice, but I did fall asleep."

Ishtar-la continued, "Thank you for your attention. We are going to study the first chapter in the book you have received. It is called "The Path of the Serpent Fire". Don't worry if you don't understand it all. We will discuss it in class; also new exercises will bring the teachings closer to your personal understanding. Open the papyrus book to page …"

She was interrupted by a Nubian messenger who arrived with terrified looks and panting breath. He looked at Ishtar-la pleadingly and suspiciously at the class group. Ishtar-la sensed the urgency of the messenger and dismissed the class.

The Nubian slave raised his face from the floor and accepted Ishtar-la's assistant's hand; he was led to a chair where he collapsed. The panting breath was recovered shortly, but his gaze still waved between

Ishtar-la and Lizla. Bowing to their teacher, the students prepared to leave.

Ishtar-la got close to Lizla and whispered in her ear, "Princess, please go to your room, but don't leave until you hear from me. I will let you know if this brings news for you."

CHAPTER 15

RA-TA'S DILEMMA

Lizla followed her teacher's advice and went back to her room to pray and meditate. By the evening, she could still not shake the image of the look in that Nubian slave's eyes. It felt like a mixture of pity, awe, and terror. Why did he pant like that, as if he were on his last breath, but did not speak until everyone left the room? Lizla was puzzled and genuinely scared now. She tried to meditate, but her mind was too agitated. She went back to her astrological chart and tried to remember what Ra-Ta had said about her cycles. They had not studied cycles in school yet; Suryananda mentioned that they would be taught later in the year, so she had to rely on her memory from Ra-Ta's reading.

How she loved Ra-Ta! She had been introduced to the mysteries by him; he was her Guru, astrologer, teacher, and guide. And the priests of Amon-Ra were the most trusted advisors of Pharaoh. If Ra-Ta went to Thebes and returned with bad news, it might mean that the whole country could be in danger, not to mention her family. Her current life cycles were: Jupiter, Rahu, she remembered. Ra-Ta had also said that she had three years more to finish her Jupiter cycle. She figured that would be coinciding with her Temple education.

Then the Saturn cycle would come, a long cycle of nineteen years. She also knew her Saturn was in the sixth house: work, enemies, war, healing, and service. That was exactly what the Goddess had said too. That was also what she had felt that afternoon in the Nile.

That contemplation calmed her down a little. Maybe disaster was coming, but it was written, so the gods would be in control.

Ra-Ta had told her once in a rare moment of tender sympathy—as he was always more severe, as it fits a member of the priesthood dedicated to the fierce god sun-Ra—that she had many gifts, but her most precious gift was faith. Lizla inwardly prayed to Isis to give her faith. But no sooner had she closed her eyes than she felt a knock at the door of her room.

Lizla was apprehensive about answering, but then she heard the sweet voice of Iris, the youngest of the Isis priestesses who had been assigned as one of her pages.

"Are you awake, my princess?"

Lizla answered dreamily, "Please come in."

But the expression on Iris's face was not comforting, as her usually sunny smile was replaced by a look of fear and her voice had a grave tone. Iris said, "My princess; a palanquin awaits you outside. Here is the message." And she stood beside the blond young man who seemed to be waiting for a reply.

As Lizla looked at him, he bowed deeply with that mocking attitude that foreigners often expressed in the presence of Egyptian royalty.

"Savages," Lizla mumbled to herself, and immediately she felt ill at ease. "Poor man, "she mused, "he is probably hungry and tired." Turning to Iris, Lizla said with an air of disdainful indifference: "Has this man being offered refreshment?"

The young man smiled and answered coldly but politely with an even deeper bow: "I have been helped, Madam."

Without looking at him, Lizla addressed Iris, "Please call Manu; he will escort me," and she opened the message roll. It only contained a brief message: "Please meet me at the Temple of Love school back entrance and tell no one where you are going. Just bring Manu." Lizla could not help a quick smile as she recognized both her beloved mentor's Ra-Ta signature and the familiar caring thought for her personal safety.

With a cold but serene look and a reassuring nod of approval, Lizla announced to both Iris and the young messenger, "We will leave at once. Just leave me alone for a minute." Then Lizla started refreshing her face make-up and combing her hair. She had not seen her master for a long time.

Then she immediately reproached herself. Could she be so irresponsible to worry about beauty at a time like this? "But beauty was what the course, the Temple of Love, was all about, wasn't it? Will they be able to preserve it through a crisis?" She thought almost absent-mindedly as she followed the slave who was doing his best to cover the lantern with a green shade while looking around him with both fear and suspicion.

Lizla wondered what any crisis measures could be applied in the sacred secluded garden of the Temple of Isis compound, in the case of an emergency. Then she remembered Isis's words and the letter. Then she pressed on, following the slave to an underground entrance behind a flowering orange tree.

The entrance led to a dark corridor with lamps fueled by olive oil, barely showing the presence of the large doors on both sides. They looked like servants' quarters. Was Ra-Ta there? Finally they arrived at one door that said in red hieroglyphics over a white frame: Healing and Operating Room. Lizla's heart jumped. Ra-Ta was in a hospital! The slave knocked on the door quietly three times.

"Who moves?" asked a guard, but Lizla ignored the question. With an imperious gesture from her small, bejeweled hand, she commanded the guard to step aside and let them in. He reluctantly opened the door. Lizla ordered Manu to wait outside and quietly entered the room.

Ra-Ta looked tired, and his skin had a greenish look reflecting the dangerous journey and the last couple of sleepless nights. His eyes shone when he saw Lizla coming in, but even then, a shadow of worry drew a frown upon his forehead.

Lizla bowed to her teacher, who quickly took her hands in his and bowed back. Her heart almost stopped as she stood up looking with concern at the hint of pain and foreboding that she saw in her teacher's eyes.

Ra-Ta made a sign to his assistants to leave. Immediately they both responded, bringing their right hands over their chests in a sign of obedience as they bowed and left.

Lizla was puzzled and curious, but she waited to be addressed by her teacher, as was the custom.

Ra-Ta smiled softly and said, "My beloved princess, thank you for coming in the middle of the night. I hope you forgive me, but what we have to discuss is urgent."

Lizla nodded, assenting to the unnecessary explanation. "Of course, but please tell me how are you? I have received this letter from you and even before, several distressing intimations of troubles to come" …

Ra-Ta's face was briefly lifted up with a sad smile and he said, "Please sit down. There is much to discuss, and we do not have much time." Lizla wanted to say that she suspected the urgency when they were meeting in the middle of the night like this, but she nodded and sat down quietly.

Ra-Ta continued: "I was in my way to Thebes on some Temple business after my short retreat, so I have not seen you. How are you? Have you started the Temple of Love classes? I barely made the initial ceremony."

Ra-Ta was impeccably polite as always, so Lizla was happy but not surprised that he was withholding his urgent news and first attending to his duties as a teacher and mentor.

"My beloved teacher," she said. "Much has happened, and yes, I did miss you! I felt your presence and guidance from far away, but how I wished I could discuss some things. But please, first tell me, are you all right? I have been having these ominous dreams and visions."

Lizla's anxious voice brought a deeper smile on Ra-Ta's face and he bent to hold her hand in support.

"My dear Princess, please tell me about it; I am sure our experiences are related."

Lizla described her descent into the lower platform of the Eastern Front of the Isis Temple and her brief but overwhelming encounter with Horus ... The strange story of Mikos and his engraved ancient coin ... Ra-Ta frowned upon it, but signaled her to continue. Lizla related then about her encounter with Psusennes, and his confirmation of the rumors she had heard from Princess Lillie and the Persian mysterious voice.

"Which rumors and which friends of Lillie? She entertains many visitors ..." Ra-Ta frowned deeper this time.

"Well, it was just after the eclipse, the day that Ketu went over Ra, when Suryananda, our astrology teacher, said that the eclipse meant a temporary setback of the Pharaoh's forces in Aswan, but that eventually the Egyptian forces would triumph."

Ra-Ta made a gesture of recognition. Ah! The eclipse, how come he did not think about that? This time he felt irritated with himself. It had happened again; whenever he got distracted with government affairs, his scholarly duties suffered. He should have been there to protect Lizla and train her in the rules of cosmic protection.

"Oh, my dear Princess, you went through all that alone? What else did he say and what happened to you?"

Lizla tried to reassure him. She was not alone anymore and felt protected in the Temple. She answered quite assuredly, "My revered master, I feel protected here, and the training I got from you was a great guidance to understand and study Suryananda's classes, as well as Princess Ishtar-la's classes."

Lizla could not avoid a tinge of pride, as she thought over her introduction to the Temple of Love's first lesson.

Ra-Ta held both his hands in his lap and smiled to himself. Venus in Leo, the true heart of a queen.

Then he replied, "Of course, my princess, you have been selected to this training because of your gifts and destiny. You also have the protection of the gods, although you seemed to have been afraid of Horus. Why? Did he look threatening to you?"

Lizla tried to remember. "No, it was that his pyramid was made of a blue light, and I could go in without problem, but Mikos was kept outside. He said it was like an electric current, like the one in the fountain."

Ra-Ta raised his eyebrows. Mikos was a Greek boy; the electric properties of the fountain were a secret of the Egyptian initiates.

Lizla reassured him as she continued, "Mikos has an Indian Guru, and he was an Initiate."

Ra-Ta signaled her to continue, "And then what happened?"

"Well," Lizla continued, "the pyramid's blue light turned to red when I went inside it. It seemed to palpitate like a heart, and then a blue eye stood in the middle. I remember that I closed my eyes because I was so afraid; also my own heart seemed to stop, so I was truly terrified. When I finally opened my eyes, the blue light was back, and someone touched my shoulder. I was told I lost consciousness. The next thing I remember, Mikos was shaking me up, and we ran back to the platform."

In spite of his age and wisdom, Ra-Ta could not contain his surprise and admiration. He was also trying to hide a bemused smile at his disciple's need to control her emotions to such an extreme.

He said, "Oh, my dear princess, once again you have been truly blessed! What a grace-filled experience! One that many wise men would dream about. Lord Horus was showing you the way to your own heart. That is why it felt like yours had stopped. But at that point, your mind intervened and in trying to understand, that is to control the situation, you closed your eyes, and it disappeared. It was your *Ka* who touched you on your shoulder. Remember that from our desert classes?"

Lizla assented, a bit ashamed now. Such a beautiful and rare experience, and she had ruined it with her need to control everything. The anxiety of the day made her feel especially despondent.

"Oh, my beloved Master, you are wasting your time and wisdom on me with my foolish ways, and maybe even attracting the wrath of the gods." Lizla's eyes were full of tears.

"Oh, my princess, don't worry. The gods understand, but Lord Horus was trying to teach you that the answers to your questions are in your heart, through meditation. Did you ask him any questions?"

Lizla remembered, "Yes, I asked him about the meaning of my visions and the engraved ancient coin."

"Well, that was your answer." Ra-Ta forgot protocol and gave his royal disciple a supportive hug.

Lizla dried her eyes and thanked him. "Oh, my dear teacher, what about your news?"

But Ra-Ta needed to hear her first. "Please tell me the rest of your story. They may be related," Ra-Ta urged her.

Lizla tried to recall, "Oh, yes, after the eclipse, there was a meditation and I saw a huge black galloping warrior coming to me, but before I could see his face, the chimes that signaled that meditation was finished sounded and the Temple doors were opened." She paused, but Ra-Ta signaled her to continue. "Then I went to the citrus grove by the western wing of the Isis Temple, those trees that connect with the Temple of Love. There I was sitting by the lake, and I suddenly overheard the conversation between Aunt Lillie, her friend Diogenes, who is Mikos's brother." At that, she could not help noticing Ra-Ta's brief frown of disapproval. Lizla continued, "I hid behind a big palm tree, so they could not see me, and suddenly I heard a mysterious, melodic voice with a Persian accent."

Ra-Ta's intentional look felt a bit severe in regard to Lizla's innocent narration. "Persian voices always sound—to our harsher desert ears—melodic, but I wait to hear the whole story."

Lizla blushed a bit. She truly had felt attracted to the musical voice, but she continued: "They were discussing the sea people, the

Nubians, the Assyrians, and other foreigners. There were rumors of war. Also, they spoke of how the Priests in Thebes may have been in contact with Nubian diplomats." Lizla ventured this last piece of information softly, as she feared Ra-Ta getting offended in support of the Amon-Ra Priests. But, Ra-Ta gave no sign of surprise or disapproval. Then Lizla continued, "Well, we had our first class with Ishtar-la, and we were studying Kundalini in the *Ka*, and she was about to initiate the Anatomy of the *Ka* lesson when the slave came in." At this point, Lizla stopped and awaited her master's comments.

Ra-Ta smiled softly. "Aren't you forgetting something? You had a dream about me."

"Who told you?" Lizla was surprised, forgetting she had shared her dream with Psusennes that afternoon by the lake.

"Someone you try to forget as hard as he tries to remember you." Ra-Ta's soft laugh brought a new blush to Lizla's cheeks.

"Oh, yes, I told my cousin. He said he knew about your trip to Thebes." Lizla inwardly acknowledged Ra-Ta's suggestion that her cousin was a bit disruptive to her peace of mind, but decide to keep silent about it.

Ra-Ta smiled knowingly and said, "Your cousin is of royal blood, a dedicated devotee of Isis, and of Egypt. I am training him both through spiritual and political counseling. He admires you very much, but he also respects you." Ra-Ta sighed. "About my trip, it was very eventful too. My slave, not the stranger you saw in the dream, woke me up with a letter from one of our loyal priests in Thebes. The priests in Thebes are wary of the war costs; it eats into their temple profits. Since they support the local population, they feel responsible for the granaries and the ownership of the land."

"But the land belongs to Pharaoh!" Lizla exclaimed.

"Yes, I know, and they know, but the Nubians don't want to know, and they instigate rebellion among the weakest of our religious brothers. In addition, some of the Nubians warlords have married well into the Egyptian aristocracy in Thebes, so they are very well connected with political power and wealth endowment. So it is not as simple as it seems." Ra-Ta's frown was deeper this time as he remained silent for a few minutes.

Lizla could not dare to interrupt again. She was anxiously awaiting every word her teacher was kind enough to share with her. She knew even that was a privilege, for people outside the highest level of the priesthood or the government rarely got this information. At the moment, she was neither, so she felt she had no right to ask more.

But Ra-Ta continued, "Narumi, my Nubian slave was killed when mapping the trip for me. As I boarded the boat for Thebes, I received a strange message from my own master, Amon-Ra-Tel, whom I had not seen in many years. He summoned me to his chambers."

Lizla was astonished. She remembered Narumi was the name of the "stranger" she had seen attacking Ra-Ta. But it was also the name of his personal slave. What did that mean? Maybe Ra-Ta did not truly know his servant … But she did not interrupt him.

"My master told me not to go to Thebes, but to hide in Psusennes's palace, while the boat with Narumi went up the Nile towards Thebes. It was most fortunate for me, at least. The boat was attacked by pirates, and they burnt it down. I have not heard of any survivors." Ra-Ta's sad look betrayed his distress in losing Narumi, and also disbelief in so much turmoil, so close to the priesthood and the royal family.

But Lizla was thinking that these events, painful as they were, coincided with her dreams and the rumors that Princess Lillie and her friends were discussing in the garden. And Psusennes—what was his part in all of this?

"Why Psusennes? Last time I saw him, he was going to Thebes to find you." Lizla wondered, thinking aloud now.

Ra-Ta continued, "Yes. He was going to accompany me, but was detained by the news of the sinking ship. News travels fast in the town of Memphis. Anyhow, he could not leave immediately, due to matters at home; when he was ready, the ship had left. That is when my master got us together. I am staying at his palace, except tonight.

My other Nubian slave, Fireas, was attacked by some strangers while he was carrying my message to you at Princess Ishtar-la's school." Ra-Ta was about to break into tears, but managed to control his pain. He realized he was being isolated, but why?

Lizla forgot all protocol and embraced him. She then tried to sound reassuring. "Psusennes will know what to do. Thank you for risking your life to come here. Are we safe here?"

"Yes, this is the Psusennes's personal residence in Memphis. He uses it for ..." He did not continue.

Lizla did not care to hear about it. She could imagine, but she said politely: "I am sure a prince of his stature may have business and trading in the city. Memphis is the link to the outside world and the Sea People, Crete, Greece, and Palestine, right? Lizla needed her mentor to feel better, so she pretended to ignore what she knew of his cousin's famous love life.

"I suppose so," said Ra-Ta, "but now I will hide in his palace up the Nile. The one with the outstanding zoological garden. Do you know it?" Ra-Ta looked suspicious to her, as she nodded with approval.

Lizla laughed softly, "My father used to take me there when I was a child. Yes, please hide there; in the meantime, what should I do?"

"For now I would like you to act like you know nothing," Ra-Ta answered. "Let Ishtar-la continue her lessons. Incidentally, she mentioned she was planning to use the zoo for training. I will see you there. Just be careful."

Lizla agreed and bowed to her master. Then she covered her head with her beaded Persian silk mantle and, signaling Manu to follow her, she went out to take the palanquin back to her apartments in the Isis Temple compound.

Chapter 16

The Hall of Stars lesson

Lizla slept peacefully for the first time in a week. She felt it was great to see her beloved mentor and to find out that the problem with the Thebes priests was merely one of regular politics. But why were the Nubians being slain? That was the last thought that crossed her mind before she fell asleep.

She then had a dream. She was back in time as a little child following her father and his page around the wonderful zoological garden that Psusennes's father had built by the Nile, one hundred miles south of Memphis. She had always been both afraid and fascinated by tigers. There was a particular one whose fierce growl shot rivets of terror through her spine, but she couldn't help going by his cage. It was such a beautiful cat, she thought once, when she had seen it sleeping. In her dream she was again facing the fierce feline, and it seemed again to be peacefully sleeping. But it was not. When the tiger saw her standing there, it began to growl. But this time she was not afraid. She went up to the cage and starting petting him. To her surprise, the cage door opened, and the tiger came out, as it often happens in dreams. Soon the tiger's face changed to Psusennes's, who was smiling at her. Suddenly the light of the morning sun woke her up.

Lizla pondered about the meaning of the dream as she was dressing up for the astrology class. She felt unusually hungry, so she dressed quickly to join the school breakfast line. After breakfast, she went up to the Hall of Stars. She had eaten a good breakfast and felt better. But still she had felt somewhat annoyed because she slept too much and had to leave in a hurry, forgetting her books and her Jyotish calculation tables.

The Hall of Stars astrology class was full, as today's lecture was central to many other disciplines. Also, Suryananda had a reputation for being an extremely accurate astrologer. It was hard to get a reading with him, but being a student of his class gave reading priorities.

The theme of today's class was: "Planetary Powers and their Relationships". This was a subject in which the Indian Masters excelled. Even the professional Egyptian astrologers that were consulted by the royal family or the wealthy merchants took classes in India or under Indian masters to deepen their understanding of this mysterious science. The Indians called their astrology Jyotish, which means in Sanskrit "the Light of God." This sacred knowledge was the privilege of sages and Brahmins and contained a compendium of different sciences: astronomy, astrology, mathematics, medicine, psychology, magic, and religious studies.

Soon Lizla noticed that Mikos was sitting in the front row and that his eyes were absorbed in the flamboyant Indian Master. Suryananda was the name that the astrology teacher was given when he took his training, back in Benares, under a famous Indian sage called Brighu. Suryananda means "the bliss of the sun" and when he got into his beloved subject, he truly shone with a passion for classic astrology. His fiery red hair would fly with his emphatic messages. His appearance was royal and bursting with such energy, as if the spirit of Ra himself had possessed him. Lizla admired that, but also kept a respectful distance from those dramatic expressions. They were fine, but she personally felt more comfortable with the measured and self-contained expressions of her Egyptian teachers.

Mikos was taken over with both the drama and his own hunger for knowledge and understanding. Lizla remembered Mikos' story of his discovery of the engraved ancient coin, when he had discovered his own healing gifts and vocation and mysterious references to the Prince of Peace. She had forgotten to ask Ra-Ta about it, but made a mental note to bring it up in one of Suryananda's classes. An event so important must have a place in the stars, she mused silently. Also, she remembered there was a Zodiac under the lamb on the Prince of Peace side of the pouch. Lizla wondered if Mikos had ever discussed the issue with Suryananda. Annouk-Aimee had mentioned that Mikos had been invited to join Suryananda on his trip back to India, so probably Mikos had some form of mentorship agreement with the Indian Master.

The teacher said, "We saw the eclipse last week as an example of planetary war. The planets are living beings, devas, we call them in India. A deva is a divine being, a great angel or a god. The planets have a personality, powers, and territories which are different from one another. Also, their influences can be positive or negative on a human life, depending on many natal chart conditions." Suryananda stopped to look at the class for any reaction. But his audience was enraptured with his talk, so he continued in the same passionate tones and dramatic gestures, as he strolled back and forth, while he pointed to the solar planetary system chart on the wall.

"The power of the planets affects every living force on earth. Their energies, together with the sun's energy—which in Jyotish is seen as another planet, although it is truly a star—provide input into our own energy. Our own energy comes from the *Ka*la Purusha, the soul of mankind, and is our own, as an individual manifestation of the divine energy of the creator. We are not always conscious of this. The process of attaining this divine energy consciousness is called the path to Enlightenment."

"The planets and their powers act upon the individual energy of a human being." He paused to ask a question of the audience: "How many here have heard about Prana?" Most hands went up. Suryananda smiled to himself. He was both pleased and proud to teach such a well-educated audience. Obviously the gods of wisdom must be pleased with his work and had blessed him, he thought with inward pride and thankfulness.

"The prana is the individual energy that controls our bodies, minds, and hearts, and it is a physical manifestation of the divine energy in a human incarnation. It runs through a collection of structures called Nadis. The Nadis are the subtle nerve system of the physical body. In India we called this body of light Shakti; in Egypt you call it the *Ka*. It is made of electric energy and thus responds to influx of energy from many sources. The planetary powers feed the prana, particularly through the sun and the moon. Actually, inside a human body"—and he pointed to another chart on the wall that contained a human frame with a detailed map of the *Ka* structure—"the three major nerves or channels of energy are these: the Ida (sun), Pingala (Moon) and the Shushuma which we will discuss in another class." He paused and reviewed the looks in the audience. Then he said: "Any questions so far?"

A timid hand in the audience went up. It was Mikos. "Pardon me, sir, but in our medical classes we have heard that the energy of the prana came through the breathing process."

Suryananda's arms went up in a gesture of emphatic recognition. "Excellent question, Mikos. And you wonder how come the Sun and the Moon can influence it?" Mikos assented and sat down. The crowd was a bit surprised at the Greek boy's question, their eyes going back and forth between him and the teacher.

Suryananda paused a second to continue the explanation: "You said very well that you learned this in the school of medicine. However, that is why we just show it here, only as it relates to the planets. In a school of medicine you probably will go deeper into chakras, glandular systems, the flow of psychic energy, the organs of the body and so forth. All that is true, but beyond the scope of this class on the power of the planets. Suffice it to say that the prana is affected by the Sun and the Moon as it goes through the process of inhalation and exhalation. In the Shushuma nadi, where the seeds of destiny—which are called samscaras—are contained, there are also psychic centers. These centers of energy are affected by the planets too. But this anatomy of the spirit is better explained in the Medicine School healing classes and also in the Temple of Love schools."

"What we need to focus on here, to understand the power of the planets, is their influence on our psychic instruments—the mind, the heart, the ego, the senses. The influence of the planets on these centers is responsible for our likes and dislikes, feelings of despondency or enthusiasm, ability to attract or reject the opposite sex, our disposition to accumulate wealth or resources, the ability to absorb wisdom and knowledge, and our capacity for procreation and parenting, among other things."

"As you can see, understanding the influence of the planets in their respective houses and within a person's cycle scan gives us a deep understanding of a person's destiny. This is the joy of Jyotish, a gift from heaven and the planets to the faithful human beings that revere wisdom and knowledge. Any questions?"

No hands went up.

Suryananda smiled and pointed to the chart on the left. It was a zodiac with the twelve signs displayed. He then said, "Please let us engage in an exercise. Since we discussed the planetary powers and how they affect the psychological body, you need to learn personally how to experience its influence, so that this knowledge is not just theory for you. Because each one of us is born out of two parents, the concepts of Karma and fate affect us quite physically. We use this knowledge not only to align our personal and political decisions according to the Kala Purusha, the spirit of the times framework. It also and most importantly helps us to understand our own inner selves, and that cannot be learnt in books and classes. It takes inner work. How many of you meditate daily?"

A small group of hands went up. Lizla was happy to see that Mikos joined her and a group of about one-fifth of the class.

Suryananda sighed and asked again, "How many of you have learnt formal meditation techniques?" Almost all hands went up. Suryananda continued in a more grave tone of voice: "I hope this class and the rest of the classes in this sacred temple of knowledge guide you to the practice of searching for inner wisdom. You will find out that the experience of governing countries, armies, classes, temples, or businesses requires much clear vision, moral strength, and freedom from fear and stress. There is only one way to keep yourself together through all things, even in peaceful times—a peace which nobody can guarantee for long, anyhow. This unfailing method is the way of faith, discipline, wisdom, and understanding."

The princes, priests, and other educated members of the audience picked up their alertness at this fiery speech. They were not used to being chastised, but Suryananda did not give them time to revolt. He added quickly, "In order to use the knowledge of these sacred sciences for our own benefit and the benefit of the people we are in charge of, either as students or subjects, we need to understand the workings of the planets in ourselves first and then in others. And the most important planets for each one of us are the ruling planet of your birth time and the moon; also the ruler of the Moon sign at birth. Please take a copy of your natal chart and find the ruler of the rising sign. In Sanskrit it is called Lagna Rasi. There, please find the position of the natal Moon. The sign where the Moon is deposited is also found in the chart you have called Chandra Lagna.' Please take a moment and look for those while we have a pause for refreshment. Let us be back in fifteen minutes."

At that moment in the back of the auditorium, large curtains were opened, and a stream of servants came up with blank papyrus sheet books and ink and reed pens to take notes. Behind them there was another group of female slaves carrying trays of fruits and refreshments. The books and refreshments were put on the different tables. As quietly and gracefully as they had entered, the group of slaves bowed to Suryananda, awaiting further instructions. Suryananda signaled the head of the servants' group to come closer to him.

When he arrived, Suryananda whispered in his ear, "When I raise my hand, please close the curtains on all the windows to leave the room dark except the one on the eastern wall, where the deep blue glass filters the sun. Close that window too, but leave at least one foot open in the middle so blue light filters into the dark room. At that time, announce to the musicians that they can begin, only the lyres—they already have my instructions. Later on, I will clap three times. At this time the musicians should stop, and all the curtain windows should be opened to filter the light in. Do you understand all of this?"

The Egyptian servant leader assented proudly as he brought his right hand to his left shoulder in sign of obedience. Then he bowed and signaled the slaves' group to follow him. They left immediately, and Suryananda went up to the food table to join the students in a brief refreshment of coconut milk and dates, his favorite snacks. Once again, he could not help being impressed by the quiet efficiency of the Temple servers. Very quickly and silently they had set up the buffet: a rich assortment of grapes, dates, pomegranates, cheese, honey cakes and different refreshments, including sweet wine, coconut milk, chamomile tea, and lemon-flavored water. The piles of fruits, cheeses, and cakes were set up around a beautiful garland of jasmine flowers that culminated in a centerpiece of beautiful flowers. And it all took a few minutes that went noiselessly and uninterrupted in the background.

In India—Suryananda reflected—only princes got that kind of treatment, and then it was far more ornamental with spicy foods and statues of the gods of good luck and food. Also, there would not have been wine in a Temple ... but Suryananda did not mind. He was truly thirsty after talking so much and enjoyed the quiet but efficient ways of the Egyptians, maybe a little tasteless for him, but sober enough to facilitate learning.

When the chimes indicated the end of the restful period, students slowly left their chattering groups, picked up their books and returned to their respective seats.

Suryananda waited until everyone settled down and said, "Each one of you was asked to bring your natal charts. If you don't have them with you, and you remember the information by heart, that is fine too." He gave a quick look at Lizla who had forgotten her books. Lizla blushed but could not help being impressed by the teacher's alertness and control of the class.

Suryananda continued, "In this generic chart," he pointed to an Indian Jyotish chart that was hanging on the wall, "you can see each of the zodiac signs and the ruling planet written in each box. Please locate two signs—the one that coincides with your rasi chart first house. We call that the Lagna or ascendant. It is called ascendant because it was the sign that was rising on the horizon (that is in the east), at the time of your birth. It indicates the time of your birth, which is also your first breath. It is the most personal and individual of your astrological data. The rising star ruling the house of your birth has more to say about your identity than any other astrological factor."

He looked around for questions or comments, and then he continued: "The other sign you have to identify is the one where your natal Moon is located. Please do that research now and write the name of both planets in your exercise books." He paused and went to the refreshment table for a cup of water. He loved coconut water, but it always left him feeling thirsty after he had to talk in public. The desert climate was dry enough, he mused, as he drank a full cup of lemon-flavored water.

Returning to the stage, he asked the students "Are you ready?" Most people raised their hands. "Now for the personal side of this exercise. As we saw before, the planetary spirits radiate their energy on the earth and on each other. Those vibrations that affect us most are the ones associated with the two signs we have selected. There is a mystery behind this that cannot be explained in human terms. The mystery is related to the secret but universal mechanism of magnetic attraction between our individual Karma and the time of birth, with its individual planetary set-up. The Kala Purusha has a complex system of inner workings like most of nature. The laws of attraction and repulsion between planets, people, and their combining relationships with time and circumstances, influence the scripts written by the gods, whose powerful minds and hearts can orchestrate the complexity of these 'coincidences' beyond our understanding. We must take on faith what the holy sages teach us, because as you will learn, when we follow the rules they give us to make our calculations, they prove remarkably accurate."

He waited for the students to finish their research, then he continued: "Now that you have identified your ruling life planet (ascending) and your mental ruling planet (the ruler of your Moon sign), we must get to meet them personally."

A whisper of surprise and fear rippled through the room. Suryananda laughed aloud and continued, "Please don't worry. We will not bring them into the auditorium." The students joined in his laughter now. "No, we will meet them personally in the privacy of your own hearts. It will be a 'dharana', which is a Sanskrit word for a contemplative exercise. As the room gets darkened, you will hear the sound of the lute music, which will help to create a quiet environment. I will lead you into meditation, and you will have the opportunity to let your ruling planet talk to you. We will do the same for the Moon sign later. I will not disclose the nature of the planets or their characteristics. That will come later, so you don't let your imagination interfere with your actual experience. Any questions?"

Annouk-Aimee was sitting behind Mikos. She felt compelled to raise her hand. "Is this safe?" she asked. The other students were either skeptical or sneered directly at what it seemed like a naïve girl's comment.

But Suryananda raised his own hand to stop the ripple of comments. Then looking at Annouk-Aimee with his wise burning eyes, he smiled softly and said, "Do not be afraid to ask. That was an excellent question. Yes, normally I would be concerned with that too. People in my country propitiate the planets with mantras, gifts, acts of charity, and so forth because it is always dangerous to open your spirit to powerful forces. That is why I asked if you knew how to meditate. I am sure your meditation teachers had given you specific instructions in how to protect yourselves when you open up to cosmic forces. But in this case you are safe for two reasons: first, your ruling planet is in you already. It feeds your energies, so all you are doing is to meet him consciously. Remember that the planet is following God's will in helping unfold his creation, of which you are a part. The second reason is that

I will lead the meditation session, and so you will receive specific instructions on obtaining the necessary protection from harming force, should there be any. Besides, this sacred Temple is purified daily by the priestess of Isis's rituals, prayers, and chanting, so it is not a welcoming place for demons. They prefer battle fields and carnivals," he laughed softly. "Any more doubts or questions?"

No one responded, so Suryananda raised his hand and immediately, the auditorium window curtains were drawn, leaving the room almost totally dark except for a band on the center of the eastern window where a blue light filtered the rays of the sun through dark blue stained glass. The calming blue light flooded the room and was soon accompanied by the soothing sound of several lyres.

Then Suryananda said, "Now close your eyes, and let us all together recite the Isis invocation."

The sonorous voice of a selected group of chanters initiated the first verse of the Isis hymn. The students responded to the chant. When the hymn was finished, Suryananda's voice was the only sound they heard in the semi-dark room as the lutes had stopped with the end of the chant.

The teacher said, "Now take a deep breath, breathe deep in and then long out. Repeat once again. Now let us do the OM chant."

The lead chanters initiated a powerful OM that filled the room with electrifying vibrations. The OM reverberated inside Lizla's soul as she felt her heart expand, and she experienced the feeling of going very deep into herself as the sound seemed to clear her mind and senses.

Suryananda interrupted the fourth round of OM and said very softly, "Now go inside yourselves and listen to your *Ka* as he shows you the voice of your ruling planet as it may speak to you in the sanctuary of this sacred atmosphere we all have created."

A deep silence fell, and soon the soft lyres resumed the lulling meditation music, filling the darkened room with ripples of caressing waves, floating the students' souls into the mystic stillness.

Lizla had not brought a copy of her astrological natal chart, but she had memorized enough of it due to her desert training. Her ruling planet was Saturn for the Moon sign and Saturn was also the ruler of the rising sign. In addition, her Ketu rising accentuated her psychic nature; that much she knew. But she did not feel comfortable with meeting either one of them.

Suddenly she saw herself in a deep forest. Tall trees, higher than the temple columns surrounded her. In front of her there was a trail going into the depth of the forest. At its entrance there was a man with strange blue eyes. His hair was blonde and long, reaching down to his waist, but his beard was almost white. Before she could speak, the strange man took her hand and, putting a finger on his mouth to indicate silence, led her along the trail into the forest. The trail ended on the edge of a cliff that opened up into an abyss. The strange man looked into Lizla's eyes and without releasing her hand he announced, "I am Ketu." Lizla trembled at these words: wasn't he a demon, was he going to throw her into the abyss? But Ketu smiled and his luminous blue eyes shone with further intensity. "Do not fear, Princess. I am here to bring you a message from your destiny. Look down here."

Lizla opened her eyes, but she was no longer in the room. She was standing in front of this abyss where clouds and fireworks of cosmic proportions were displayed. It was like universes were born and dying in seconds.

Ketu pointed down and solemnly said, "This is the cosmic pattern of creation and destruction. The mission of wisdom—my mission and yours—is to discover all this, and by this knowledge glorify the handiwork of the Creator." He then disappeared as Suryananda had made the music stop, and the chanting group initiated the Isis invocation.

Dreamily, the students left their meditation state by joining the chant. When it was finished, Suryananda said, "Take a deep breath, move your fingers and toes, and when you are ready, open your eyes." Next the big curtains on all the windows were drawn open, and the radiant light of the desert sun flooded the auditorium, spreading in a magnificent array of colors as it was filtered through the stained glass windows.

Lizla looked at Mikos and saw he was entranced by the beauty of the room. Lizla smiled to herself. She too felt the touch of grace putting a tone of glory in the room. It was typical of deep meditation experiences. Sometimes she felt it in the food too, but she would never tell that to Mikos. He was such a rational thinker!

In addition, she had much to contemplate. Her experience has been unusual. Why did she not see Saturn? Was Ketu her ruling planet? She would have to discuss that with Ra-Ta next time they met.

Suryananda's instructions took her out of her reflections: "Pick up your writing materials and describe the experience you just had. Please write until the chimes ring again." For the next ten minutes the room was quiet with the students' contemplative journaling.

Twenty minutes later the sand clock weight agitated the chimes that announced the exercise was over. Suryananda looked at the students and asked them, "Do you have anything you want to share, any questions, surprises, concerns?" Lizla raised her hand.

"Reverend Teacher, I do have a question. I did—which is not unusual—have a very strange experience." She paused as a ripple of soft laughing broke for a moment the solemn atmosphere. "I know this is not everyday fare, but I was expecting to see nothing or at least a vision or image from my ruling planet …"

Suryananda put a finger on his lips. "Your Highness, please don't say his name. Ruling planets are most personal. Also and particularly for rulers or people in a position of power and privilege, you need to learn to be cautious about inner data, particularly in public."

Lizla continued, a bit chastened but still determined to get an answer: "What I saw was not my ruling planet but another visitor, an old man with a white beard, strange blue eyes and blonde long hair."

Suryananda raised his hand to suffocate the "Ahs" and "Ohs" from the auditorium floor. "Please continue," he said. "What else happened? Did he tell you his name?"

"Yes," Lizla said, "he said his name was Ketu."

Suryananda did what he never allowed himself to do when dealing with astrological knowledge: he jumped. That provoked many eyebrow-raising and muffled comments. Lizla was feeling quite self-conscious now, her original blush turning to livid pale.

Suryananda composed himself and addressing Lizla, he said gravely, "That is the south node of the Moon; it is truly a geometric point in space although the legends point to a more colorful origin." He paused and was happy to see that Lizla assented, as she was well aware of it. "The south node of the Moon and his disturbing potential was discussed in the class that we observed during the eclipse. Was he threatening you?"

In spite of Ketu's being recognized as the lord of mysteries, he was also reputed to create mischief and occult, hard-to-unravel problems to the people or nations that displeased him.

"No," said Lizla. "Actually, I was concerned too when I heard the name, but he took me very gently to the border of a precipice and there he showed me down in it, how the worlds evolve and universes appear and disappear." Lizla's eyes almost closed dreamily as she remembered her astonishing vision. The class was suddenly very still in quiet admiration.

Suryananda ran his hand through his long, matted hair, absorbed in thought. "Do you remember Ketu's position in your natal chart?" he asked.

"Oh yes," Lizla said, "It is exactly on my ascendant."

"Aha" the sage concluded. "That was it. And it is an important rule for us to contemplate. The planet that is closer to the ascendant is the third one most important for us, after the ruler of the Moon sign and the ruler of the rising sign. Because your first house or rising sign represents your personal destiny, a planet close to you personally tends to filter his energies to you more closely too, so when you opened up to contact the planetary powers, he showed up. Also, he seemed to have a powerful message for you. In addition, Ketu rising makes one psychic. Thank you for sharing. We will continue our lesson on the meaning of planetary powers after lunch. Class dismissed."

The lunch pause lasted two hours. The heat of the desert sun made these noontime hours hot, and some rest was indicated before continuing. The students left the room silently as it was prescribed in golden hieroglyphics in every wall of the auditorium.

Lizla felt some strange glances directed at her. Between the power of the experience, her embarrassment at sharing, and the feeling of being scrutinized, she hardly touched her lunch.

One look was more insistent than any other. It was her cousin, Psusennes. He had heard Ra-Ta, his master and spiritual mentor, comment on Lizla's gifts, but today he had the opportunity to see his cousin in another light. Beautiful as ever, she had stood firm sharing her experience, her brief blush turning to pale embarrassment at the reactions from teacher and from students alike. But now he had seen her exquisite glow serene and shining like a bright new lotus out of the Nile, Psusennes thought to himself. He could not stop staring at her. Lizla caught him and already irritated with the events of the morning, she silently returned his annoying stare with a ferocious look. Her anger made her even more fascinating in his eyes.

After the lunch pause was over, the class returned to the Hall of the Stars. Suryananda had organized more charts in the front of the auditorium. But once the students were placed in their respective seats, he pulled a slow curtain over the charts.

"Before we continue, we will recap and answer questions. We were talking about the planetary power and how the planetary energies intersect with our own. That is all part of the original energy of the Creator as it manifests in this, our planet Earth. Any questions?"

This time Psusennes raised his hand. His tall, athletic figure and his reputation as a warrior and favorite of the court ladies provoked some muffled comments and some malicious glances. But he stood alone, trying to keep his eyes away from Lizla, as he respectfully addressed the Indian sage.

"You mentioned the planets as divine beings and as agents for the will of the Creator. What about our own gods: Horus, Ra, Isis, and

Ptah? Don't they have any part in the Creator's play and if so, why do we pray to them?"

The bold question was unexpected, and this time electrified the audience. There were Greeks and Cretans, Egyptians, Babylonians and Hebrews plus the Indian sage and his daughter Lakshmi sitting next to Lizla. Many they did resonate to the question, "But what about our own gods?"

Suryananda smiled and asked him to sit down. Then he replied, addressing the class, "That is another excellent question, and it also helps us to continue with the next part of our lesson. But before I answer it directly, let us consider the skies."

He pointed to the above ceiling where the constellations were painted in many colors over a deep blue background.

"Those are the stars constellation that made the zodiac. These are the path of Ra (the sun), in his imaginary road—which represents our own point of view—around the earth. The signs of the zodiac are ruled by the planets. The signs are the twelve subdivisions of the zodiac, from Aries to Pisces, named after the constellations that constitute their background." And he pointed to the shining points of light on the ceiling that marked the shape of the constellations behind each sign.

"These constellations are owned by certain gods. In India we call them Devas (divine beings). In other traditions they are called angels. But it is a question of translation only. They are the divine forces of the Creator in action. Does that answer your question?"

Suddenly, an atmosphere of unrest, mistrust, and religious zeal was disturbing the minds and hearts of the students. Suryananda felt it too and wondered if perhaps he had gone too far with his explanations for a single class.

Psusennes found he had more questions than answers. He took a quick look around him and saw some signs and looks of confusion too. They were all from different countries and cultures. They all had different gods. But there was only one sky ... how to understand that?

He also felt compelled to get up again to take a look at his lovely cousin. At this point he felt irritated with himself. He was acting like an infatuated teenager. So in answer to both his confusions and his desire, he raised his hand again. His handsome figure dominated the auditorium, but he ignored the longing looks from the ladies and the envy of the men when he stood up at Suryananda's invitation, all the while without taking his eyes off Lizla.

Suryananda was an experienced teacher. He knew how to restrain emotions in front of this class, but he could not help a bemused smile and a quick look at Lizla, who was seated next to Lakshmi, Suryananda's daughter. Lizla looked back and blushed when she felt the burning look of Psusennes, agitating her mind against her will.

Lakshmi took Lizla's hand as a sign of friendly support and whispered in her ear, "Be careful. I don't think my father believes you are blushing about Ketu." Lakshmi could not contain a giggle.

Lizla had had enough embarrassment for one day. She turned around and gave her cousin a furious look of reproach. Again Psusennes felt her disdain adding another link to the claim of affection he was feeling for her. He had never felt like that about a woman. He felt he could be her slave forever if she only gave him a smile.

Suryananda needed to control the silent drama that had different ripples of reaction among the students. But instead of dismissing the class in the midst of confusion and possible gossip, he inwardly prayed for strength and inspiration. Immediately he saw the face of his beloved Guru, Brighu.

Brighu smiled and said, "Continue with the class. This is the time to talk about divine power, not to fear the demons of the flesh or of the spirit."

Suryananda put himself together and addressed the class, "Let us hear what the prince has to say. He is a well known devotee of Isis and a remarkable Egyptian warrior. He has won brilliant military campaigns for the Pharaoh and also devotedly supported these Temple Grounds. This auditorium was built with his wealth and his own slaves support it. We are grateful. But we are here to learn and to learn is to expand our minds. Please, Prince, speak."

Psusennes took a deep breath and, making a supreme effort to avoid staring at his cousin, he pointed to the stars in the ceiling. Then he voiced his concerns about the multitude of gods and the simple face of the zodiac constellations.

"Whose power commands our lives? Who is the Creator? Didn't the gods create the stars themselves? And is not man a spark of divine light incarnated in flesh?" His heart ached, and his mind burned as he pronounced the last statement with great force. His passion resonated through the audience.

Suryananda answered, "My beloved prince. Thank you for your questions. Those are most precious questions. They relate God and man in the true link of philosophic wisdom. I will give you the answer from India, which is my tradition, but you will see, upon meditative contemplation, that the answers in your own hearts do resonate with the true teachings of every religion." And he made a sweeping gesture with both arms, signaling he included the whole assembly of multinational students. "There is only one God, the Almighty. We call him Brahman. But this divine power manifests through different forms according to the five divine functions. Those are: the creator, the sustainer, the destroyer, the concealer, and the blesser. Each of these forms has a different God name. The most important are the first three: The first is the Father or the Creator. We call him Shiva, you call him Nun. The Hebrews call him Jehovah or Yahweh. The second power is the son or Word incarnate that takes human form every cosmic age to correct the ways of men into dharma. We call him Vishnu. You call him Osiris. The Hebrews wait for him as the Messiah. He is the Prince of Peace. The third one is born of the other two and has the function to impart wisdom, grace, and understanding. He is called Brahma in India, Horus in Egypt, and Jupiter in Greece. Do you understand?"

Silent expectation ran through the room. Suryananda added, "Man is born as the living image of the Creator. In him there is a will who partakes of divine will or Shiva, a heart which is part of divine love—Vishnu, a mind which carries the power of Brahma. These forces impel man to act, to love, to think. These are the manifestations of the Divine Creator in the flesh as you were asking. The planets belong to the different gods and in their presence and movement; they affect these forces in man. But that it is the subject for another class. I believe we had enough for one day. Class dismissed."

Lizla looked at Mikos who was also puzzled by the explanation.

He came close to her and asked, "Is this the Prince of Peace in the engraved ancient coin? Next time I will ask." Lizla nodded as she left the Hall of Stars auditorium. She could still feel Psusennes's burning look as she glanced back. With an imperious gesture of disdain, she walked fast to her apartments.

Chapter 17

Psusennes's Confusion

Psusennes's emotions were in turmoil as he left the Hall of Stars. He did not know if he could accept Suryananda's explanation. It seemed very much a systematic view of Heaven, just like the accounting records the managers of his state granaries put on his desk every week. So impersonal! If all the gods were the same with different names, how can one feel true devotion to any one?

Psusennes had been fortunate to be the son of a beautiful princess. Younger sister of Ramses IX, Neferti had died when her first son Psusennes was twelve. Psusennes had worshiped her all his life. She had the most beautiful dreamy sweet eyes and a soothing melodious voice that brought comfort to his childhood's little hurts and early cruel disappointments. She was his refuge as his father was a famous general and favorite military aide of the Pharaoh. It was Pharaoh's friendship that allowed Psusennes's father to marry his beautiful younger sister. He had been devoted to her until Neferti's untimely death as she gave birth to a daughter.

Psusennes grew up in the constant care of his father and the memory of his mother. It was her that inspired his devotion to Isis. But for him, it was all so personal. That was one of the reasons why he felt so unsettled. The other one was his cousin Lizla. He could not figure her out. She had an exquisite beauty and the royal manners of his own mother. Lizla even looked like her, as Neferti had often commented when they were playing as children in the zoological garden. But Lizla had a proud heart and a steady mind. "She could be a good ruler someday, and certainly she is in the royal ascension line," he thought to himself. But why did she have such a grip on his heart?

Psusennes had had many love affairs; maybe his reputation was a problem with his studious minded cousin.

And there was also Altamira. A third reason to be upset. He found out she had had lied to him; she was not pregnant. And she was being capricious besides being deceitful. Maybe the rumors in the palace were right: she was cruel with her slaves, too. He had heard those rumors before, but he always discarded them.

"How frail is the human heart," he sang to himself as he remembered a poem he used to read to his first girlfriend, a long time ago. She had eventually married a Babylonian prince and moved away, but Psusennes had always a soft spot in his heart for her.

But now, somehow his current strange attraction for Lizla and the apparent irritation his presence provoked in her, made him feel so sad and vulnerable. He decided to go back home to his estate up the Nile where the famous gardens with the zoological park would surely provide relief to his exhausted nerves. With a heavy heart, he called his servant Zahur and asked him to bring him back his chariot with fresh horses. Zahur was surprised to see his normally cheerful master in such a despairing mood. But he was very discreet, and silently he followed his lord and took his place by his side on the chariot.

The ride through the desert was long and silent; the only sounds were the galloping horses traversing the burning sands at a great speed. Psusennes had taken the reins himself and was intently whipping the horses into greater speed. Holding fast to the rails of the chariot, Zahur could not help but wonder what the urgency of the trip was. The clear skies of the lower Egypt spring were soothing to the spirit, and the winds on their faces seemed to act like a welcome fan on the burning-hearted Psusennes as he sped his chariot with a firm grip on the reins and a deep frown on his face—which Zahur observed with some concern.

When they arrived at the zoo park state, before going to his palace, Psusennes instructed Zahur to put the chariot away and give the horses food and water. Then he went directly to the orange grove that surrounded the Isis chapel. He wanted to go inside and meditate when he overheard two familiar voices. He soon recognized them: Altamira and Ra-Ta.

The conversation concerned him and the Nubian problem. Altamira had gone to see Ra-Ta as she had heard that the Egyptian sage had gone down to Thebes on a political mission. Her real reason for visiting the sage was to find out what he knew about her relationship with Psusennes that had grown cold recently. Altamira blamed Lizla for it, but could not address the issue directly. So she pretended to be concerned with the political situation as her parents had moved to Thebes for retirement.

Ra-Ta was polite but distant. His position as a celibate monk of the Holy Order of the Ra religion made him keep a safe distance from women unless they were his disciples—who were normally men with the exception of Lizla and a long time ago, Lizla's pious aunt, Neferti, who was the late Psusennes's mother.

"The prince is in Memphis in the Astrology school. He will be back shortly," were Ra-Ta's final words to her as he politely but firmly declined to give any information about the prince's confidences to him, his spiritual master.

Psusennes was infuriated. He took a few minutes to calm himself and, passing behind a column at the entrance of the chapel, he quietly entered and sat to meditate. But Ra-Ta had seen him. He had noticed the heavy atmosphere on the prince's aura as he entered the temple and decided to let him alone. Once again, as he had done many times, he gave thanks to the gods for a fulfilling life, away from the complications of court, politics, or romance.

Psusennes felt the soft breeze of the fans on the high ceiling of the chapel. The flavors of aromatic candles and incense and the pink waves of light that entered through the western window proved a soothing mantle of relief on his burning mind and confused heart. Slowly, he raised his eyes to the life-sized image of Isis, carved in soft rose granite that towered over the main altar of the chapel. Long garlands of jasmine flowers streamed down from the ceiling, forming an aromatic background tapestry behind the statue.

The soothing perfume and soft light coming from the stained glass windows made the exquisite form of the statue even more beautiful. Her face shone with compassionate eyes, to which Psusennes was used to praying since childhood. But today the face turned into Lizla's face. The statue had been carved using his own mother as a model for the goddess. The eyes that he remembered were tender and supportive. However, this time the look of disdain he had received from Lizla seemed to shine from the beautiful statue.

This felt like another stab at his already wounded heart. Why was she so cruel? She did look like his mother, after all, she was her niece—but only today, at the magnificent display of courage Lizla showed, he discovered that her spirit also resembled Mother's. Psusennes felt hot tears rolling down his cheeks.

Always the warrior, he was not challenged even by this. He had not cried since his mother died, and his many love affairs had mostly given him joy, excitement, and sometimes surprise or fury. But his feelings were deep and confusing now. What to do? The thought of truly surrendering to a woman's charm had never occurred to him, the most sought after prince in the Pharaoh's court. But when he looked into his heart, he realized his feelings for Lizla, while passionate, had a far deeper connection. Like his own mother, who died of childbirth after some weeks of rigorous fasting to protest the Nubian invasion, Lizla represented what he loved most about his country: the ma'at, harmony, order, honor, and beauty.

He decided to go to his spiritual advisor, Ra-Ta, and ask for advice. But first he needed to refresh and eat something. That would clear his mind, or so he hoped.

He soon found out they did not. Psusennes had an uneasy frugal dinner before he retired to his chamber.

After a restless night, and a turbulent morning meditating in the chapel, he dressed himself in his best clothes and decided to approach his old master.

Ra-Ta was currently a guest in his disciple's palace. He had always been an honored guest in their home, but nowadays his apartments were strongly guarded by the palace's security legion. The rumors of hostile politics and the rebellion of the Thebes priests had not affected Memphis yet, but Ra-Ta, as the main priest of Amon-Ra in Memphis, could soon be contacted and forced to make a choice. So Psusennes, Lillie, Diogenes, and Ishtar-la feared. At their request, the sage had agreed to hide in Psusennes's palace. Another reason to find refuge there was that Psusennes and his family had strong family and business connections in Thebes. Most of the trade down the Nile and into the Mediterranean was financed by the Thebes and Memphis commercial alliance. Psusennes, and particularly his father, were both admired and feared by these merchants. Their combination of wealth, political power, and connection to the military forces of Pharaoh that Psusennes' father commanded, made the family practically untouchable by the tremors of Nubian influence in Thebes. They were needed and respected by both priests and the Nubian merchants.

Ra-Ta understood and accepted his disciple's gracious hospitality. He felt a bit constrained by the constant security guards, but he left that circumstance to the gods, as he did everything else.

Early that morning Ra-Ta heard his dear student Psusennes at the door. He rose up and went out to greet him.

"Oh, my prince, what shadow of sorrow kept you awake?"

Psusennes could not hide anything from his spiritual teacher. Yet he felt it difficult to discuss emotional issues with him or with any other man. Also he knew of the high regard that Ra-Ta had for Lizla.

So he fumbled to give an answer. He could only come up with a dejected look.

Ra-Ta smiled and patted his disciple in the back. He was aware of most of the problem. But he expected Psusennes to speak first. His patience bore fruit as Psusennes sat on the chair next to Ra-Ta and sighed.

"My beloved teacher, I see you like a holy figure and father, and it is in this trust and confidence that I come to you." Briefly he described the events at the astrology class to the priest. Ra-Ta listened attentively and when he saw his disciple was about to break up into hot tears of anger and frustration, he rose up and started to walk, pacing the room quietly to give the young man a chance to compose himself.

Then the priest said, "Lizla was your mother's niece. She is also a very beautiful woman with a proud Leo Venus."

Psusennes interrupted without thinking, "The heart of a queen."

Ra-Ta continued, surprised at the interruption. Psusennes was always a model of courtesy. "Yes she has the heart of a queen, which is what she is destined to become eventually. For that reason she needs a man in whose heart she can find a throne too." Ra-Ta smiled significantly and awaited the young prince's reaction.

"Oh, but she does, I mean she will, I am sure of it. I have known many women, but no one who obsessed me like that. I even see her face in the Isis effigy; I hope it is not a sacrilege."

Ra-Ta smiled with sudden softness. "Love is never a sacrilege, my dear prince. But as you mentioned just now, you have known many women, and that may make your cousin a bit distrustful of your ability to see the sacredness of love." Ra-Ta paused for a few minutes, absorbed in thoughtful contemplation. Then he added, "It seems, however, that the fates have many connections between you two. Such a marriage would bring a political alliance that would help heal the problems in the land."

Ra-Ta was aware that his disciple was listening, but he was mainly thinking aloud.

Psusennes jumped up. "Normally I would agree, my revered priest, but I am in love with her. I don't want a political alliance. I want her to love me, too!" Then he paused and looked at Ra-Ta to seek sympathy or counsel or some form of assurance that there was a solution to his problem.

But Ra-Ta was serious. This was an important lesson for his pupil. Also, the future of Egypt might depend on it. So he looked deeply into Psusennes's eyes and said, "My dear prince, you have distinguished yourself in battle? Has anyone else in your family?"

Psusennes was surprised by the question. His family military record was well known. "My revered priest," he answered with pride and candor, "I have had the privilege to serve the divine Pharaoh with my sword and my chariot on several occasions. My father commands the closest legions of Pharaoh. You know I am from a military family."

"Very well," said Ra-Ta. "You know that to conquer in battle requires courage, patience, perseverance, and faith, correct?"

Psusennes assented with curiosity, wondering where the priest was going.

"Well, my prince, here you have a bastion of strength, your cousin Lizla, Princess of Egypt, initiate in the Isis Temple, a formidable tower of beauty, power, wisdom, and beauty. Do you think she will surrender her virtue easily?" Ra-Ta's eyes were gleaming with a meaningful smile as he put his hand gently on the shoulder of his distressed pupil.

"Surrender her virtue, my lord? But I am planning to marry her," Psusennes cried.

Ra-Ta nodded. "But that is permanent surrender, my dear friend. Also you would share her throne."

Psusennes fell into despair again. He shook his head sadly. "I don't care about the throne." Then he immediately took control of himself and corrected his own words: "Of course I do. I am willing to give my life for it. Any true Egyptian would."

"And you don't think Lizla is a true Egyptian?" This time the priest's question had a mischievous tone in his voice.

"Of course I do. She is impeccable, almost like Isis herself. She will be a magnificent queen someday." Psusennes imploded with passion.

Ra-Ta nodded again.

His disciple added, "Oh, now I see what you mean. To conquer this priceless tower I will need the virtues of a warrior."

The priest approved and added emphatically, "And the skills of a lover. You have demonstrated both in the past. Now destiny calls you once more for the most important battle of your life."

Ra-Ta's voice turned grave, and he gave the prince a deep look, full of compassion and endorsement. "My prince I know you are up to it, but it will not be easy. Neither will I make it so. Lizla is my precious disciple, too. It was the last Pharaoh's direct command to me on his deathbed, to be supremely careful of her education. She has a royal destiny ahead of her. I admire her reluctance to choose a partner carelessly, at an age when most girls dream of romance alone." Ra-Ta's eyes were full of admiration as he remembered the valiant trials Lizla had endured during her dessert training.

Psusennes was silent for a full ten minutes. Then he rose from his seat and kneeled in front of his teacher. "My beloved master, please give me your blessing for this quest. I can see I have been favored by the gods to be born in this wonderful time and country, and I have the privilege of teachers like you. I will not fail." And with these words, he bowed his head as Ra-Ta put his hands on it and chanted a litany of blessings.

CHAPTER 18

THE ZOO GARDEN PALACE

Lizla woke up early in the morning and attended the early Hatha yoga class. She loved those Hindu exercises. Then she went for breakfast and joined Mikos for the *Ka* anatomy class in the Temple of Medicine. Ishtar-la had been requested by Ra-Ta to assign Lizla some classes in medicine. He felt it would round out her education and help to develop her healing ability.

Lizla was happy to talk to Mikos. Although his need to question everything and find rational explanations for mysterious matters were silly in her eyes, his intelligence was dear and refreshing. She also noticed that—almost against her severe will—she truly enjoyed the company of the opposite sex.

Mikos's timid glances of admiration revealed feelings of tenderness, which did not have the fiery intensity of her cousin's Psusennes's passionate staring. She could handle her relationship with Mikos, that she knew. She was not sure she could manage how to relate to Psusennes. Also, she had become friends with Mikos's sister, Annouk-Aimee, and his brother Diogenes. Somehow in running away from her cousin's ardor, she realized she was getting closer to this Greek family.

The thought disturbed her. Was she running away from her own people? What kind of a queen would do that? She was destined to lead Egypt, not Greece. Was she running away from her duties and destiny by running to this Greek family? The thought disturbed her greatly until she felt the sweet voice of her twin *Ka* whispering in her ear. Yet the message of her twin *Ka* was not reassuring.

"Maybe you are running away because you are afraid of your own emotions."

Lizla dismissed the thought. She was no coward.

But in matters of love …? They called for a courage she was not sure she had.

"No. You are wrong," she quickly answered her twin *Ka*, but even to her own ears her voice sounded unconvincing.

When the medicine class was finished, she went back to her apartment to get her books for the Ishtar-la class. Instead she found a letter on her night table. Iris apologized that the carrier slave had insisted on the letter being deposited on the princess's room and not in Lizla's attendant's hands, as was usual.

Iris was nervous, thinking perhaps this was a reflection on her performance, so she ventured timidly, "Is there anything wrong with my service, Your Highness? The Temple authorities selected me for my good records as well as personal compatibility. But if there is something I can improve, your wish is my delight."

Lizla stroked Iris's soft shining hair and smiled, "Don't worry, it was nothing like that. But this must be highly confidential."

With that she retired to read the letter. It was indeed confidential. Ishtar-la had received warnings from the Temple security office to move her classes up the Nile to the estate of Psusennes's family. Ra-Ta was also hiding there until the disruptive news from Thebes offered fewer threatening scenarios.

Lizla felt her heart going all the way up to her throat. She had to sit down and take several deep breaths before she gathered enough strength to read the missive again. An unusual streak of panic sent chilling waves up her spine. Stay at Psusennes's palace? For how long? Would he be there, in his own palace? Lizla felt really threatened until she read the second paragraph. The prince was assigned by his father, who was Pharaoh's commander of the Egyptian Royal Guards, to go to Tanis, where the palace had been threatened by further Assyrian rumors.

"Is he going as a commander or as a spy?"Lizla wondered for a moment, but soon with a disdainful shake of her head, she tried to erase her cousin from her mind.

He had been there quite often after that ridiculous scene he had made in the Hall of Stars. But Lizla couldn't stop wondering why he was leaving now that he could be getting closer to her? Did Suryananda confront him, after the class, for his silly behavior? Or maybe Ra-Ta had advised him against her? Ra-Ta was a celibate priest and quite jealous of her commitment to her studies and to her royal destiny. But he liked Psusennes.

Lizla was intrigued by all of this, but she felt better. Maybe this was good. The palace grounds of Psusennes's family were beautiful, and the zoological gardens contained many beautiful memories of her own childhood. Lizla remembered fondly the beautiful walks with her father, Ramses IX, and his sister, Neferti, who was Psusennes's mother. Lizla loved Neferti. How could her son be so obnoxious? Lizla frowned with this last thought. But Ra-Ta seemed to think highly of her cousin. And that comment from her inner *Ka* about being afraid of her emotions! She dismissed it again with another shake of her gorgeous jet-black hair.

She paused in front of a large mirror, and looked at it with apprehension. She did not have the heavy breasts of Altamira, but she had grace and dignity. And her face did not look so bad. Actually it resembled Neferti, as her father, the late Ramses IX often had commented.

And her cousin thought he could turn her into another Altamira? Never! She said it with emphasis.

She said that last word aloud, making Iris erupt into the room. "Anything wrong, my lady?"

"No, my dear Iris, just some people's heads; that is all." Iris sighed with relief. Her Highness was right. Except that here at the Temple grounds Iris had found a sanctuary of order and beauty that fit her perfectly.

Lizla looked at Iris and smiled to calm her down. "It is not you, my dear Iris. You make a great priestess in this holy ground. And when you blush like this, you truly look like a flower." Iris bowed deeply to her mistress and departed.

But Lizla called her back: "Iris, I need you to help me pack. Call Ila-Re and prepare for me a set of clothes, shoes, and jewels for a two week trip."

"Where are you going, my lady?" Iris ventured, not wanting to sound too inquisitive.

"Up the Nile, my dear Iris, up the Nile, same climate." Lizla responded with an enigmatic smile and left the room.

The following morning a messenger from Ishtar-la was waiting for Lizla at dawn break. She was ready, and with the help of Iris and Ila-Re, she finished dressing. Soon, after taking an early breakfast, she left for the Memphis seaport on the palanquin that her teacher had sent for Lizla. At the royal deck, a beautiful vessel was always ready to fulfill the traveling needs of Pharaoh's family. It had extreme security too. Ishtar-la had used her influence and the presence of Lizla, heir to the throne, as a reason to find room in the royal vessel for herself and her small group of disciples.

When the tide was favorable, the ship left the dock. For security reasons, the six members of the Temple of Love class were allocated to different cabins. Ishtar-la's instructions to everyone were to meet at lunchtime in the boat cafeteria.

This was a luxurious room. Silver chandeliers on every table matched the silver cords attached to elaborate tapestries from India and China, hanging from the ceiling, which served as powerful fans. There were child slaves from Nubia and some from the north, Lizla thought looking at the fine golden curls of a couple of them. The children slaves did the light tasks like serving water and pulling the silver cords of the ceiling fans.

Ishtar-la said a short prayer to bless the food and gave her five selected disciples a mysterious look.

CHAPTER 19

LIZLA GETS HER FIRST LOVE LESSON

Ishtar-la started by reassuring her disciples. There was nothing to fear, just a precaution and a break from the more rigid schedule of Temple life, to go into nature to study the workings of the *Ka* within a more relaxing environment. She noticed Lizla seemed worried, and after lunch she decided to have a talk with her.

At Ishtar-la request Lizla confided that she was puzzled by Psusennes's behavior in the Temple of Stars.

Ishtar-la listened pensively and responded, "How do you feel about it?"

"Well, I think" … but Ishtar-la raised her hand to stop her.

"I said how you feel about it?" and she smiled softly to invite Lizla's confidence.

The princess stopped and reflected for a minute. "I felt embarrassed. Everyone was laughing at us. Also, he has no right to make a claim on my attention. He has all the women he wants," Lizla said with a note of sarcasm that she felt surprising coming from her mouth.

Ishtar-la put her hand on her disciple's hand and responded tenderly, "But you have not told me how you feel about him."

Lizla was surprised again. "Yes, I did. I find him obnoxious."

Ishtar-la smiled again. "That is an evaluation, right? I don't mean his behavior, but his person. He is quite attractive, isn't he?"

"Of course he is. Ask any noble lady from Thebes to Tannin," was the exasperated response.

Ishtar-la decided to try once more: "I am asking you, specifically."

Lizla paused for a moment and took a deep breath. "I know what you mean. Of course he is attractive." She smiled shyly now. "Once, actually the last time I saw him alone, he even stole a kiss from me. He caught me by surprise. Then he immediately left."

Ishtar-la was the one surprised by this revelation. "He did? And what did you do? Did you slap him or shout or anything?"

"No, I was surprised. I just stood there, frozen. Actually, no, I confess I felt pretty warm. Maybe ashamed!" Lizla's eyes looked at her teacher to see her reaction.

Ishtar-la squeezed Lizla's hand and looked into her beautiful wistful eyes. "My dear princess, don't you think it may have been interpreted as a welcoming response? If you have been waiting for him to kiss you, and he caught you by surprise like this, and then left, what would have been your reaction?"

Lizla thought it over: "Well, I guess, the same, but that was not my intention …"

Ishtar-la smiled again and, releasing Lizla's hand, she shook her head. "Ah, my friend, we all tend to interpret other people's intentions from our own point of view. It seems that Psusennes has indeed fallen in love with you, and he may even hope for it to be mutual. Is that so impossible?" Now, it was Ishtar-la who had a question in her eyes as she looked at her puzzled disciple.

Lizla shook her head in defiance and announced proudly, "As if there are not enough Altamiras in the world."

Ishtar-la now laughed freely. "My dear princess, your cousin is a great warrior, but also he is well acquainted with the opposite sex."

"I'd say," retorted Lizla with unexpected fury.

"What I mean," Ishtar-la laughed softly, "is that he knows very well you are not Altamira. He does not lose sleep over her, but the other way around. I think that was the last rumor I heard."

"Exactly!" Liza cried. "That is why I was so embarrassed at the Hall of Stars lesson."

Ishtar-la was serious now; she held both Lizla's hands in her own and said with patient determination: "My dear princess: that is a very good lesson for you. In your position you will always be in the public eye. How you react to it is crucial in your job. Also for that reason, it is important to be aware of your feelings so they don't betray you, either in private or in public.

"I was trained in that since childhood," Lizla responded pensively.

"Yes, and now it is time to apply it. I truly suggest you meditate on this. This man is a member of the royal family; he cherishes you and respects you. He is very powerful, devout, and committed to his ideals. Not to mention his handsome looks! Someday you will need a husband to share your throne, both in the land and inside your own heart. If you feel it is too early for you to make such a decision, which is fine, you are very young still." Ishtar-la concluded by waving to two of her other disciples who were just arriving.

Lakshmi and Annouk-Aimee were approaching as they made a walking tour around the boat. Ishtar-la rose from the bench she was sharing with Lizla and invited her three disciples to join her.

"Let us go up to the captain and ask him to give you a navigation lesson. Would you be up to it?"

The girls were excited about it. They were in school after all and enjoyed the magnificent views of the Nile shore that was flanked with statues of ancient Pharaohs. The Giza pyramids were becoming smaller by the hour as the boat proceeded steadily south, propelled by many agile row men who insured a steady speed up the river.

Lizla rose up and took a deep breath against the mighty wind. The seagulls surrounded the ship, and the fishermen stood still watching the royal boat pass by. They bowed reverently at the passing of the flag with the Pharaoh's crown of the two kingdoms. Lizla dreamily waved to her future subjects as she kept on chewing on Ishtar-la's last words: Yes, indeed, being a queen would be her first duty, so she would ask Isis's guidance about her future. She smiled, remembering that in Psusennes's premises she would also meet her beloved master: Ra-Ta. As usual, she felt secure and protected again. Then, following Ishtar-la, she joined the group as they headed for the captain's cabin.

The trip lasted a few hours, and by the time Ra was returning home in the western horizon, the boat had arrived at the man-made seaport that Psusennes's father had built beside the river's natural bend flanking the north border of his state. The group was received by a group of servants from Psusennes's palace, headed by the head housekeeper. She had made sure adequate accommodations and classroom settings had been duly set up and furnished for Ishtar-la and her privileged pupils.

After a sumptuous dinner, at which the group marveled, as they had been used to the excellent but frugal meals of the Temple of Isis, Ishtar-la took the group by a path down the garden that led to the zoo. The garden path was streamed with flowerbeds of many colors, while a canopy of gardenia vines covered a large part of it. The canopy finished in front of a large fountain that was built around a life-sized statue of Isis and Osiris holding hands. Neferti had gotten permission from the temple to add electric wiring to the base of the fountain. Although electricity was a secret guarded zealously by the priests, sometimes it was allowed to be applied to a divine statue. At dusk, high streams of water colored in pink, blue, purple and yellow chirped happily around the statue, creating an otherworldly effect that contrasted with the austere silence of the many stars in the deep blue firmament.

Lizla could not help thinking about Psusennes and how this wonderful site would have been a daily visit for him. She imagined him as a child chasing light bugs by the fountain, or later in early youth, stealing kisses from adventurous princesses, as the rumors went. That thought made her feel quite irritated, and she did not notice a quiet figure that was looking at her intently.

Suddenly she heard her name, in the voice of a beloved figure.

"Ra-Ta," exclaimed Lizla, and she extended her hands to meet her Guru. As he approached, she bowed to receive his blessings. Then, at his invitation, she sat by the small wall at the fountain border. He sat next to her and looked at her in silence.

"How are you, my beloved teacher? Do you have any news from Thebes? Are you safe here? How long will you stay?"

Ra-Ta smiled to see her youthful enthusiasm had forgotten all care. The gardens were dark, yet there was no way he could assure privacy. Anyone could be listening.

So, ignoring her questions, he asked, "How was your trip, my dear? Are you learning much in Ishtar-la's classes? I heard you had an interesting astrology class. I wish I could have been there. I admire Suryananda very much, both as an astrologer and a teacher." Ra-Ta could not help a smile, anticipating Lizla's response.

"Pardon me sir, but if you were not there, who told you?"

"Someone that was highly impacted by the event. In fact, I think it may have changed his life forever."

Lizla was really puzzled. "One of your disciples? Does this have anything to do with my Ketu experience? Suryananda asked for sharing and that is what I did. I had no idea …"

But Ra-Ta interrupted her by putting a finger to his lips to signify silence. "My dear princess, you had a long journey, and tomorrow the classes will begin at noon. Please come by my cell at ten a.m., and we can discuss it."

So they walked in silence back to Psusennes's palace, and Lizla went up to her room. The lamps were low by her bed, but she could see an exquisite tapestry covering the floor. It looked Persian, Lizla thought. High over her bed hung a canopy of transparent linen that acted as a mosquito net. Several vases with flowers were displayed around the room. A table with refreshments, fruit, and sweet wine was covered by a big dome of translucent blue glass.

On it she found a letter and a small box. She opened the letter. It was from Psusennes. He begged her to forgive him for his imprudence at the Hall of Stars. He then declared in passionate tones the depth of his love for her, his determination to plead for her love "for eternity", and he abjectly begged her to accept "this humble gift from a disconsolate cousin."

Lizla frowned both at the letter and the avalanche of mixed feelings that it caused in her. Then, with tremulous hands, she opened the box. Tears came to her eyes when she saw the contents. It was a beautiful ivory pendant with a golden chain for a necklace. The pendant opened, and inside it there were two paintings that she had seen often—much larger—in the Tanis palace halls. The one on the right was her own father, Ramses IX. The one on the left was Neferti.

Lizla felt her head spinning at this sight. But she was, as Ra-Ta said, very tired. She went to bed and had a strange dream: She was again by the zoo and still trying to see the tiger. As she approached the tiger's cage she was expecting a ferocious growl, but instead she saw the tiger was older and quite tame. He had a junior female tiger by his side and two wonderful small kittens. Lizla got in and tried to pet the kitten. She advanced with trepidation, but the parent tigers did not move. So she picked up the smaller kitten and started caressing it. When the kitten turned around to look at her, it had a sweet disposition that melted her heart with tenderness.

Chapter 20

Altamira's Wedding

As was his custom, whenever possible, Ra-Ta had risen early to take a stroll around the magnificent gardens that surrounded Psusennes's palace. Normally he would go to the zoo and watch the servants feed the horses, tigers, cobras, and gazelles. They even had a large lake where crocodiles and rare lotus flower ponds were commingling in peaceful coexistence. Springtime was a time for renewal and to reflect on life. Ra-Ta felt there was nothing like nature to celebrate the rhythms of life. That rhythm had unfortunately accelerated in not so harmonious tones lately. Psusennes had left the palace with a heavy heart but embracing with fierce determination his decision to be the ruler of the heart of his beautiful cousin. Together with Ra-Ta and his connections at Thebes, they had also provided Altamira with a silver bridge to avoid her future interference with his plans.

The plot brought fruit as this morning a magnificent vessel, owned by one of the Nubian princes, arrived at the dock of the private seaport of Psusennes's estate. The emissaries had sent special invitations for Psusennes, Lizla, and Ra-Ta to the celebration of Altamira's wedding to Arshaka, the prince of Nubia that had family relations to the king of Babylon, after whom he was named. This powerful prince was reputed to conspire against the throne of Egypt and his powerful Babylonian connections made him a notable but feared visitor in the Pharaoh's court and especially among the rebellious priests at Thebes. But Altamira's hurt from Psusennes's rejection and her natural ambition made her overlook the political implications. She wanted a rich and powerful husband to show her old lover that she could do better without him.

Unbeknownst to her, when her parents received Arshaka's emissary asking for an audience, they never knew it had been orchestrated by Sabola, a wise man and faithful servant of Ra-Ta in his previous temple at Thebes. Sabola was never a priest, but he had an excellent education, and he spoke Babylonian, Greek, Egyptian, and Nubian. Ra-Ta trusted him completely as an emissary and as a frequent tutor of princes both in languages and religion. He had been offered by Ra-Ta as a welcome gift to Arshaka when he arrived in Egypt five years before. Through Sabola's careful service, Ra-Ta managed to keep an ear on Thebes's politics and the priests' partial rebellion.

Some of the Thebes priests opposed the rulership of Pharaoh over the two kingdoms as they owned much of the land around the huge monasteries. They wanted to keep the grain and money produced there for their own work and service, but in loyalty to Pharaoh they had to produce tribute to the crown, pay for Pharaoh's wars, and the government costs. That was the right thing to do, and ma'at had supported this view for centuries. But in the last forty years, agitators from Nubia and Babylon, jealous of Egypt's riches and their unified kingdom, had infiltrated the southern temples at Thebes and provoked rebellion. Their long-term goal was to secure the throne of Egypt for a future Nubian king.

Ra-Ta was lost in his thoughts when he saw the slender figure of Lizla walking up to his apartment to keep their morning appointment. Ra-Ta returned to his place promptly, and he arrived almost at the same time as his disciple to the door of his room. He asked her in and offered her a seat and refreshments. Lizla accepted politely but did not eat much, as she'd already had breakfast.

Ra-Ta looked at her and smiled: "Well, my dear child, what were your questions yesterday? I have much to tell you, but most of it is confidential, so the palace gardens in today's times can be non reliable grounds to discuss such matters."

Lizla nodded in understanding. Then she said, "What was all the commotion this morning? I saw a great luxurious boat, with a Nubian flag, at the prince's dock. Are we being invaded?" she joked, as she knew well it was a royal yacht and not a military boat.

But Ra-Ta's face was grave in answering: "Not yet, my dear princess."

Lizla looked at him, alarmed:" What do you mean?"

Ra-Ta took a deep breath and continued: "You will soon receive an invitation to a wedding through a Nubian emissary."

Lizla's eyes were wide open in wonder. "Who?"

"An old friend of the family, actually a young one, I may say, whom you may remember: Altamira. She is being married to the Nubian prince Arshaka."

"The king of Babylonian's nephew?" Liza was astounded. "I thought he was here for the Babylonian's ambassador's son's wedding."

"Indeed my dear, princess, that was the official reason for his trip. But he is also looking for his own connections with the Egyptian ruling classes."

Lizla thought for a moment. "Altamira's father was my youngest uncle. He never married her mother … that hardly makes her a royal princess in Pharaoh's house." Lizla added with a mixture of pride and disgust.

"Oh, my dear princess, royalty should not be stained with arrogance, but adorned with noble thoughts," Ra-Ta answered reproachfully.

Lizla lowered her eyes as she answered her teacher: "What I meant …"

But Ra-Ta interrupted. "I know, but that is close enough considering her adoptive parents' wealth."

Lizla nodded again. "Yes, they are rich enough; she grew up with us as a child and was rather spoiled. I am sorry if I sound proud again, but she was cruel, impetuous, and frivolous. I never cared to be her friend." Lizla was guarded but firm.

"Yes, I know, and I agree. Incidentally, she does not like you either. She came to me a couple of weeks ago; she wanted news from Thebes, but she was also inquiring about you and Psusennes."

Lizla was suddenly enraged. "She did not! It was surely all Psusennes's fault. He made a fool of himself in the last Hall of Stars class." Lizla was agitated and also confused.

Ra-Ta put his hand on his disciple's shoulder. "You must learn not to judge too harshly my dear. Oh, you are very young, but unusually mature for your age. You may want to add patience and compassion to your many virtues. They will serve you well as a queen, and as a woman."

Lizla felt chastised again. But she realized her cousin provoked intense emotions in her which she could hardly understand sometimes.

"Psusennes is seriously in love with you. He wants to marry you; that is why he left. He can't stand your rejection. So he went up into battle. I hope he does not pay too dearly for his pain." The priest looked at Lizla for an answer, but her confusion was too great. She could hardly raise her eyes from the floor.

Then the priest continued: "Well, the Altamira news could help your cousin in his goals." He ventured a look at Lizla, who slowly raised her wonderful eyes to meet her teacher's. There was a trace of tears in them that Ra-Ta found hopeful. But he continued with the political discussion.

"The situation is still undecided at Thebes. The Nubian princes and specifically the merchants of both countries all look to our country's riches and our advanced civilization with envy and no less greed. What they think is that the Pharaoh's absolute power over the land can be easily obtained by usurping the throne of Egypt with one of their princes."

"But the Pharaoh rules over the land and the people as their master and god," Lizla interrupted. "The people will not accept a foreign ruler. It is precisely our family-like country set up and our respect for honor and tradition that the Pharaoh's crown of the two kingdoms sustains and represents!"

Ra-Ta smiled to himself and added soberly, "Exactly. You have the perfect picture, but they don't know that. They are used to power conquered to sword and to wealth by trading and slaving. In truth, they perhaps could conquer the Egyptian throne and for a while support the situation, since our structures are solid, but it will all eventually deteriorate. That is why unity in the land is important. For us and for the civilized world. You see, Egypt is more than a great granary to the world. It is also an advanced civilization which the scholars of the world and the brightest students grace due to its stability, refinement, and respect for the law." Ra-Ta was thinking aloud now, but he was well aware that his words resonated with his favorite disciple.

Lizla was deep in thought, too. She remembered the goddess's early prophecy about becoming a healer to the country divisions. Maybe the hour had come, or it was certainly approaching.

"Is there anything we can do to help?" she asked.

Ra-Ta took a deep breath and looked at her silently for a few minutes. "My dear princess, the situation is still confusing, as apparently everything is all right. The Pharaoh is secure in Tanis, the schools are safe, the rebellion in Thebes contained, and no enemy has threatened our borders. But underneath they are moving. You see, Altamira's wedding will give the Nubian prince Arshaka, who is a close relative of the king of Babylon, serious proximity to the Egyptian royal family. They have infiltrated like this through marriage or business alliances, all over the south, particularly in Thebes. What Egypt needs now is a secure royal line that ensures legitimate succession, from truly divine Egyptian Pharaohs. Only that can promise the priesthood and the people the stability, military power, respect for tradition and religion, for a state based on true ma'at."

Lizla was thinking aloud now: "My father had no male heirs, and I am the eldest. My uncle has no children from his queen. So that makes me ..."

"Heir to the throne," Ra-Ta finished her thought. "But you are also very psychic, young, and female. Arshaka is marrying your sworn enemy, so you can expect opposition unless ..."

He was interrupted by his eager disciple: "Unless I marry a man strong enough to share my throne who has the respect of both naturals and foreigners alike." Lizla was thinking aloud. "Anyone you know?" she said without lifting her eyes from the floor, a sly smile flowering her pretty full lips.

But Ra-Ta was serious. "If you're thinking about your cousin, yes! I think that would be ideal. But he is in love and resists the idea of a simple political alliance. Anyhow, you are too young to marry. Yes, not by Egyptian standards of simple age. But as a future queen, it would be best that you continue your education. But we were discussing the political situation as you asked me yesterday. Does that answer your questions?" Ra-Ta knew better than to press a sensitive issue that needed considerable contemplation from his resolute disciple.

But Lizla had a need to share her late experiences. She said, without taking her eyes off the floor, "He left a beautiful letter and an exquisite present for me." She felt almost guilty about judging him so harshly, and she showed the beautiful pendant to Ra-Ta. The priest was both moved and surprised by Psusennes's gesture.

"But that is the pendant his mother gave me on her deathbed. She made me promise he would never take if off his neck."

"She made you promise that, not him." Lizla felt incredibly surprised at her defense of her annoying cousin.

Ra-Ta's eyes looked at her with tenderness and respect. He then said: "My dear princess, you will be late for class, and I am due for a lecture I have to give in the palace's library."

"Oh, what about? I would love to attend." Lizla was always eager for learning.

"It is about the legends of the ancient mysteries. This is something someday you will discover further and teach us all. Remember the Goddess's prophecy?" And bowing farewell to the princess, he guided her to the entrance to the corridor that led to the classroom wing of the palace.

Lizla bowed back to her teacher and proceeded to Ishtar-la's classes. She still had an hour before noon. Lunch would be served at the class break, so she had some time to be by herself. She decided to take a look at the zoological garden. She went down the familiar path to the tiger's cave. But she felt desolate when she discovered that the old tiger had died, and no replacement had yet arrived. She thanked the slave in charge and gave him a silver coin. Then she decided to take a stroll by the Nile. She had a lot to think about.

CHAPTER 21

THE DAWN OF LOVE

Lizla sat down by the river and took her sandals off. She loved the feeling of the water on her feet. The currents were stronger here at the South, she noticed. The river was younger, closer to its birthplace. The waters were purer, and she once again had the memory of visits to the river for the blessings ceremonies that her father, the late Ramses The IX, used to conduct when she was a child. After the ceremony, she always managed to stay behind and dip her feet by the river. In the recently blessed waters, their shapely form seemed to melt into the Nile. She never felt closer to her father than at those times.

His reverent invocations would reverberate in her young mind, "Oh holy father of Egypt, you unite the South and the North with your life-giving grace. Grant us peace, prosperity and union, that we can honor the sun god Ra with his gift of light and the mother moon with her gift of peace and the rhythm of your tides. You are our lifeblood that keeps the desert alive to feed our hearts, our souls, and our bodies. Amon-Ra-Auml" She memorized that prayer in her heart as she felt the river current melt her own *Ka* into the eternal mystery of the Egyptian soul.

But something was different today. Her own heart felt empty and a bit frightened. Her father was no longer alive, and the cave of the dead tiger had made his absence more poignant to Lizla today. Lizla remembered Ra-Ta's teaching about the moon, how it represented the power of the mind but also ruled the cave of the heart. The tiger had always been a symbol of both courage and fear to Lizla. She had dreamt he was alive and had a family of his own. Maybe that was in the future? Right now it was empty. His cave was being cleaned up, and his memory would soon be erased. Lizla's tears made the shape of her feet under the water almost disappear completely.

She took the pendant that Psusennes had given her in farewell and opened it. How beautiful was his mother, Neferti! Lizla used to admire her so much. She had the quiet strength of her brother, Ramses IX who was Lizla's father. But Ramses had married Nubkhesed, his older brother's sister, who became Lizla's mother. Nubkhesed was the heir to the throne, and the oracle had declared the royal couple to be the legitimate next Pharaoh and queen.

Lizla's aunt had remained a source of fascination to her. Lizla remembered the Isis statue that her own father gave Neferti, his sister, in honor of her first son's birth. Lizla had gotten her first vision of Isis from the statue. Isis had looked so radiantly beautiful, like her own aunt, Neferti.

Lizla decided to get up and go to the temple. On the door she found a small package with her name on it. She opened it, surprised. How did anyone know that she would be going there? It was a message from Ishtar-la. Lizla was to return to Tanis immediately. Her mother had been taken ill and was summoning her.

In the package there was a short poem that Ishtar-la had decided to share with Lizla. It was an intense prayer to her own gods, to protect her beloved husband in battle. She prayed to Ishtar—the Babylonian Goddess of Love—to spare the life of her beloved husband, asking the goddess for he "whose burning eyes have kindled the fire of my heart."

Lizla felt tears of fear and remorse rolling down her cheeks: fear about her mother's health and remorse because the burning looks of Psusennes only had provoked pride and anger in her. Was that why she felt the cave of her heart was so empty? Maybe that was what the old tiger was trying to tell her in her dreams.

And Psusennes had taken the valiant gesture to put his life at the service of his country while she was safe and sound at the temple school. Lizla rolled down the papyrus message and put it back in the box. Then she cut some flowers from the garden and reverently entered the temple.

Lizla's psychic nature always found a welcome relief in temples. Particularly today, she felt the silence in the temple had a healing quality to it. It calmed her mind, soothed her spirit, and made her communion with the *Ka* full and complete. She bowed down to the statue of Isis and raised her eyes.

She was astonished at what she saw. She had not seen the statue since the last time she had visited this garden, when it was new. Lizla was ten years old then, shortly before her father was killed in battle. But this time, the statue seemed to be the living image of her own picture in the mirror! She humbly offered her flowers on a tray with a burning candle she picked from the altar, and looked again. The resemblance was uncanny. Lizla then found her way onto a cushion on the floor and tried to meditate. But her heart and mind were in turmoil. A few minutes passed by. The sweet smell of incense lingered with the perfume of the gardenias in her offering tray. A soft breeze touched her forehead, and its cool relief flooded her with a feeling of peace. Lizla felt the soft touch of the goddess's hand on her hair, and once again she noticed warm, salty drops rolling down her cheeks into her trembling lips. She tried to pray, but she could not.

Yet suddenly her heart was not empty any more, neither was it afraid. A strong resolve rose up in her. It was more than her looks that the goddess had blessed her with. It was a divine strength that ran through her soul. Just like the Nile, it seemed to overflow with the expansion of her youthful dreams.

She would go to Tanis and be by her mother's side and perhaps let the burning looks of Psusennes kindle her heart as Ishtar-la had responded to those of her beloved husband. Then Lizla suddenly remembered that Ishtar-la's husband had died in battle! Lizla rose to her feet. How was Psusennes?

She prostrated herself before the life-sized statue of Isis and prayed fervently.

"Oh divine Mother, please protect your son!" A sudden feeling of intense longing pierced her whole frame. Once again, she felt all alone. She rose, put her shawl around her head, and bowed gratefully to the statue. It seemed to answer back with an exquisite look of love and support.

Lizla felt courage inundate her resolve. She would go to Tanis at once. Oh, how she needed to see her mother, and how desperately she wanted to see her cousin again!

She walked back, always facing the statue, toward the temple door. Suddenly she felt a warm hand grasp hers. Its unseen owner was guiding her out of the temple. Lizla quietly let herself be led into the glorious garden.

Under the brilliant desert sky, she met the tender eyes of her cousin, who was worshipping her with his adoring gaze.

Psusennes said quietly, "I came back for you. Your mother needs you." Seeing her alarmed look, he added softly: "No, she is not ill. That was the message we wanted the spies to hear. But she has urgent political matters to discuss with you. I volunteered to escort you to the Tanis palace. Will you come, please? The royal boat is waiting for us."

But Lizla could only notice the exquisite touch of his well-shaped hand over hers. She took hold of his hand and looked into his eyes. Then she let his burning lips touch hers, feeling transported into a daze of winged dreams.

But soon she recovered her composure, put her shawl around her neck, and answered brightly, "Just let us bring Iris with us. She will help me to pack."

Holding his warm hand, Lizla let Psusennes guide her back to his palace. She had never seen a garden look so radiantly beautiful.

About the Author

Lilian Nirupa is a lifelong student and practitioner of Eastern Philosophy and Spiritual development in several traditions. She has travelled all over the world and is well acquainted with many cultures and specifically with traditions around spiritual and children Psychology.

She has written extensively for corporate best practices in Information Technology Management. She holds a degree in Education and a Masters in IT Management She currently lives in Southern Maryland, in a quiet setting surrounded by woods which she finds quite inspirational for both her spiritual and artistic pursuits. She has two grown-up sons and a one-year-old grandson.

978-0-595-45682-6
0-595-45682-0

Made in the USA